Breaking Rules . . .

"This place is such a drag," Kye complained. "Why don't we get out of here?"

"You mean, you want to finish lunch outside?" Cara asked.

"I didn't mean *that*," Kye said, laughing. "I meant leave-leave. You know, take a half day."

"Cut school?" Cara exclaimed.

"Come on, Car, let's go to the beach. It'll only be fun if you come with me," Kye pleaded.

"How will we leave without getting caught?" Cara finally asked, her palms sweating at the prospect. No one she knew ever cut school.

"We'll just sneak out the back door," Kye said. "Anyway, what's the worst thing that could happen? You're already grounded. What else can they do to you?"

"All right, let's go," Cara agreed, not wanting Kye to see she was scared to cut.

She and Kye walked out of the cafeteria, and down the hall to hide in the bathroom until the late bell rang. They almost made it to the back door when they ran right into Mrs. Hartman . . .

TROUBLEMAKER

Developed by
Elle Wolfe

This is a work of fiction. All the characters and events portrayed in this book are fictitious, and any resemblance to real people or events is purely coincidental.

TROUBLE MAKER

Cover art by Richard Lester

ISBN: 1-55902-985-4

First edition: December 1990

Printed in the United States of America

0 9 8 7 6 5 4 3 2 1

117231

CHAPTER 1

"*You* got invited to Cara Knowles' party?" Esme Farrell asked, her blue eyes widening in surprise. Nicole Whitcomb nodded her head, her brown ponytail bobbing up and down. "You got invited to *the* party of the year?" Esme continued.

Nicole nodded again and said, "Yeah, but it's not like—"

"What's up, *chicas*?" Alicia Antona asked as she sat down on the bench across from them. The three girls were in the cafeteria of Palm Beach Preparatory School for Girls. The cafeteria was crowded with sixth grade girls. Alicia opened her milk container and blew her straw wrapper at Esme. "Where's Quinn, anyway?" she asked, shaking her black curls off her face as she took a long sip of milk.

"I don't know, I thought she was coming down with

you,'' Esme said. "You're not going to *believe* who got invited to Cara's party.'' She paused dramatically.

"Esme—" Nicole began, embarrassed.

"I can't believe it! I got detention again!" Quinn McNair interrupted, throwing herself down on the bench next to Alicia.

"What'd you do *this* time?" the Cuban girl asked, sighing. Quinn always seemed to be getting detention for something. She and Mrs. Hartman, the headmistress of Palm Beach Prep, hadn't been on the best of terms since Quinn had come to PBP that fall. Quinn said it was just a "difference of opinion."

"I don't even know what it was this time," Quinn complained. "Something about my uniform, I think."

The three girls all looked up from their lunches to stare at Quinn. "Was it your socks?" Nicole asked. Quinn almost never wore the regulation navy blue knee socks. And she didn't simply wear plain white socks instead. She had an amazing collection of wild socks in every imaginable color.

Quinn stood up so they could see her socks. "Maybe," she admitted as Nicole, Esme, and Alicia started laughing.

"Maybe?" Esme giggled. "Those are definitely not navy blue!"

Quinn glanced down at her socks. They looked as if a comic strip had been printed all over them. "They're not that bad," Quinn said, trying to look serious. "Sean found them in some store and bought them for me." Quinn's brother Sean encouraged her strange sock behavior. He was always buying her the most bizarre ones he could find.

"So, who was invited to Cara's party?" Alicia asked, getting back to Esme's original comment. "You never did say."

Nicole looked uncomfortable. "I was," she blurted out before Esme had a chance to say anything.

"*You* were?" Alicia squealed. "I don't believe it!"

Nicole pulled a pink envelope out of her science book. "Here's the invitation," she said, waving it in front of the other girls. She didn't look very happy about it.

"Why did *you* get invited?" Quinn asked bluntly. "I mean . . . I didn't mean it like that . . ."

"It's okay, Quinn," Nicole reassured her. "I was totally surprised, too. Maybe her parents made her. Since they're friends with my mother and all . . ."

"Well, are you going?" Esme asked eagerly.

"You are going, aren't you?" Alicia practically commanded.

"I don't want to—especially if you guys aren't going," Nicole admitted.

"You *have* to go," Quinn ordered. "I'm sure your grandparents will want you to . . . and we want you to go, too."

"*We* do?" Esme asked in confusion. "We weren't even invited. Why do we want Nicole to go?"

Nicole looked questioningly at Quinn.

"We want to hear all about the party. So you'll have to go and tell us everything!" Quinn explained.

Alicia giggled. "Really, Nicole. It's not every day that

3

someone has a party with sixth and seventh graders—and guys!''

"It might even be fun!" Esme put in. "I heard Bobby Turner and Tyler Stein were invited."

"Patty Porter told me that only the 'cool' people in the sixth grade were invited," Alicia said, giggling.

"Well, then I can't understand why *I* wasn't invited!" Quinn exclaimed, pretending to be hurt.

Esme, Nicole, and Alicia laughed. Cara and Quinn had been fighting since Quinn had come to PBP at the beginning of the year. Cara had invited Quinn to a party on her first day of school, and Quinn had been miserable the whole time. She ended up storming out, but not before telling Cara how stuck up and snobby she thought she was. Cara had been out to get Quinn ever since.

"So you're going, aren't you, *chica*?" Alicia asked Nicole.

"Yeah, you can be like our spy or something," Esme said, giggling. "We want a full report on Saturday!"

The bell for the next period rang, and the four girls brought their trays up to the dishwasher. Then they headed for their lockers before English class.

"Esme!" Ms. Bosson called across the cafeteria. The gym teacher was the proctor on duty that day. She held Esme's knapsack up by one of the straps. "I think you forgot something!"

Esme ran back to get it. Her friends were laughing when she rejoined them in the hallway.

"I really believe you would lose your head if it weren't attached," Quinn kidded.

4

"I would not!" Esme exclaimed indignantly. "Besides, my agent would remind me to bring it to shoots!" she joked. Esme had been a model since she was five. Her work had mostly been for catalogs and book covers, but now she was starting to do shoots for teen magazines, like *Sassy* and *Seventeen*.

The girls walked to their lockers together, stopping at Quinn's first. She hit her locker right below the combination lock, and it swung open. The inside, which had a lived-in look, was plastered with pictures of her favorite rock stars, like Ziggy Marley and Prince. She grabbed her books off the top shelf and followed the others to Esme's locker.

"This stupid locker," Esme complained as she struggled with her lock. She finally got her combination to work on the third try. She held out her hands to try to stop the avalanche of books that had already begun to fall out. She piled them back on the top shelf and then checked her hair in the mirror hanging on the inside. Surrounding the mirror were pictures of River Phoenix and Kirk Cameron that she had ripped out of *Teen Beat*. There was also a *Seventeen* cover featuring a model friend of hers. Sticking out of the bottom section was a bag with clothes and Hot Sticks hair curlers that she had shoved in and forgotten about after her shoot the morning before.

"You really should clean that out soon," Nicole warned Esme, "or you're not going to be able to open it."

5

Esme looked offended. "It's not *that* bad. I know where everything is."

Quinn laughed. "Not everyone can be as organized as you are, Nicole. Besides, don't you feel needed? Esme really needs you!"

"Right!" Esme said. "I need you to grab that book and that pen over there." She gestured to the notebook and pen on the floor behind her. "I can't reach them, and if I move this whole locker's going to fall on the floor."

Nicole laughed as she helped Esme shove everything back into the locker. Esme shut the door before it all fell out again.

Then Nicole went to get her own books. Her locker was as neat and organized as she was. All of her books were standing straight up on the bottom. Pictures of her horse, Simon, were hanging in a row on the door, and an extra pair of riding jodhpurs were folded neatly on the top shelf.

The warning bell rang just as they got to Alicia's locker. She had covered the entire inside of it with fuchsia and neon green contact paper. Her friends always joked that it was a great way to wake someone up in the morning.

The girls made it to class just as the final bell rang. Mr. Holmes wasn't there yet, but almost all the seats were already taken so they had to sit in the front row.

"Good afternoon, girls," he greeted them, walking in. He cleared a space for his books on the desk. Mr. Holmes was every PBP girl's dream guy, and they were always leaving him little gifts before class started. Today he had to sift through three apples, some homemade brownies, two cards, and a few flowers in order to even find the desk.

"This morning we're going to discuss the assigned reading—chapters one through four in *A Day No Pigs Would Die*," he said, as he opened his own copy. "Open to page twenty-four, girls. Virginia, can you please read the first two paragraphs?"

Everyone quieted down as Virginia read from the book. "Can anyone explain those paragraphs?" Mr. Holmes asked when she had finished.

Quinn raised her hand. English was her favorite subject and Mr. Holmes was her favorite teacher. In fact, the English department was the main reason she had transferred from public school in Nueva Beach to PBP.

Mr. Holmes didn't call on her. Instead, he spotted Esme trying to hide behind Alicia. "Esme? How about you?" he encouraged.

Esme felt terrible. She really liked Mr. Holmes, not to mention the fact that he was totally gorgeous. But she hadn't read the chapters. In fact, she didn't even have her book open to page twenty-four. Nicole was just trying to whisper the page number to her when there was a knock on the door and Mrs. Hartman walked in. Esme breathed a sigh of relief.

"Saved by the knock!" Quinn whispered, and Esme giggled.

"Hey, who's that?" Alicia asked, looking at the girl behind Heartburn. The newcomer had long dark hair hanging loose to her waist. She was wearing a black

7

T-shirt underneath her uniform jacket, which was covered with laminated buttons of rock stars. Her black lace-up boots and slouch socks were definitely not in uniform. And neither were the hot pink lycra leggings that ended right below her knees. It was obvious that Mrs. Hartman was giving her a break because this was her first day. The headmistress was usually very strict about the girls' uniforms.

"Girls," Mrs. Hartman began, "I'd like you all to welcome Kye Baldwin. She just moved here from New York City."

Everyone stared at the new girl. She stared back defiantly. New girls were very rare. Quinn was the last new student in the sixth grade, and she had started in the fall.

"You can take a seat, Kye," Mr. Holmes said with a smile. Mrs. Hartman whispered something else to Mr. Holmes, and was gone. Kye walked directly to the back of the classroom, and sat down in an empty desk in the corner.

"Maybe you should sit up front for a while, Kye," Mr. Holmes suggested, "until you catch up."

Kye looked annoyed, and pushed back her chair with a loud scrape. "Why don't you sit here by Quinn?" Mr. Holmes continued. "If you have any questions, you can ask her. And you can share her book until you get your own."

Kye walked to the empty desk on the left of Quinn and threw her books down with a loud bang. She sat down, crossed her legs and her arms, and stared at Mr. Holmes with angry green eyes.

8

Quinn looked at Kye, waiting for her to move her desk over so they could share a book. Kye didn't move. She just stared straight ahead.

"What an attitude," Alicia whispered, not too softly.

"Back to work, class," Mr. Holmes said. "Where were we?" He opened his book again. "Quinn, will you please move your desk next to Kye's so she can follow along."

Quinn looked up sharply. Was Kye's desk cemented to the floor, or what, Quinn thought to herself. She was sharing *her* book, so why did *she* have to move? Quinn slid her desk over to Kye's. She hit it with a bang.

"Watch it!" Kye hissed. Quinn glanced at her.

"Sorry," Quinn whispered.

"Teacher's pet!" Kye hissed back.

Alicia was right, this girl really did have an attitude problem.

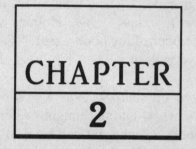

CHAPTER 2

"Great!" Quinn muttered sarcastically. "I have gym with her, too."

"What?" Esme asked, rummaging through her over-stuffed gym bag for her sneakers. "You have gym with who?"

"That new girl, Kye," Quinn answered, tugging her green and white gym uniform on. "She's in our gym class."

"She doesn't seem very friendly," Esme said, holding up one sneaker triumphantly. She dumped the entire contents of her bag on the floor to find the other shoe.

"She wasn't," Quinn said. She wrapped her gym suit belt savagely around her waist. "And the worst of it is that Mr. Holmes asked me to help her. He wants her to study with me a few afternoons a week, until she gets caught up."

"That's what he wanted to talk to you about after

10

class?'' Esme asked, putting on her sneakers and trying to shove the rest of her stuff back in her bag.

"Yeah, and Kye seemed about as pleased about it as I am," Quinn admitted. "I don't know what her problem is, but she's definitely got one!"

"All right, girls! Let's go!" Ms. Bosson, the gym teacher, yelled into the locker room. "Get a move on!"

"Just a sec, Quinn," Esme pleaded. "I'm almost ready."

While Esme finished tying her hair back, Quinn sat down on the bench. When they finally walked into the gym, they were a few minutes late. Luckily, Ms. Bosson didn't notice because she was busy welcoming Kye and explaining their routine to her.

"Okay, girls!" Ms. Bosson shouted. Ms. Bosson almost never said anything unless she was practically yelling. It must have come from being a gym teacher for so long. Most of the girls liked her, but they all wished she would speak a little more softly once in a while— especially when she was standing right next to them. "Today we're going to run on the track!" she yelled. "But first we're going to do some stretches in here."

She proceeded to lead them through some basic stretches to loosen up, so that no one would pull any muscles when they went out onto the track. Quinn noticed that Kye was hardly moving, but Ms. Bosson didn't say anything. "Cara," she yelled instead, "try to put a little effort into this, please!" Cara hated gym, and always did everything half-heartedly.

The whole gym class walked down to the track, where

11

they were loudly commanded to run at least a mile—or four times around. Quinn and Esme started jogging right away. Kye and Cara were among the last to get started. They ended up running next to each other.

"Do you guys have to run a lot?" Kye asked between breaths.

"Usually, once a week," Cara admitted, fighting to breathe. "I really hate it!"

"This is the pits!" Kye agreed, huffing and puffing.

They ran a lap silently, except for the sounds of their ragged breathing. Quinn and Esme breezed by them at the beginning of the second lap. Quinn was chatting with Esme about something, and Esme was laughing. Cara and Kye looked at each other.

"That girl is such a goody-goody!" Kye exclaimed, motioning to Quinn's back. "What a brown-noser!"

"Really!" Cara agreed, without exactly understanding what Kye meant by that. Quinn was always in trouble about something or other. Most of the teachers, except Mr. Holmes, disliked the way Quinn always spoke her mind. But Kye seemed to think Cara was cool, so she wasn't going to say anything that would make her think otherwise. "Mr. Holmes really loves her!" Cara added, knowing that it was the truth, and knowing that it made her sound as if she agreed with Kye about Quinn.

"How many miles is she going to run today, anyway?" Kye asked sarcastically. "Does she show off in every class?"

"She'll probably do at least two miles," Cara said,

beginning to enjoy her role. She always welcomed a chance to put Quinn down.

"This is totally ridiculous," Kye said after a few more minutes of huffing. They hadn't even done a half mile yet, and some of the girls had gone four times around already. "I really don't want to do any more!"

"Me, neither!" Cara agreed. "We can't just stop though."

Kye looked at Cara and smiled. She stopped suddenly and fell to the ground. "I think I hurt my ankle."

"Ms. Bosson, come quick!" Cara yelled, standing next to Kye.

Kye was clutching her ankle when the gym teacher got there.

"I think she sprained it," Cara diagnosed.

Ms. Bosson helped Kye stand up. She stood hopping on one foot. "Try to put some weight on it, Kye," she directed.

Kye cried out in pain as she stepped lightly on one foot.

"Okay, Kye, you're going to be all right," Ms. Bosson said loudly. "Cara, why don't you help Kye to the nurse's office. You probably just need to put some ice on it and rest for a few days."

"Come on, Kye," Cara directed. "Lean on me."

Cara and Kye were almost back to the main building when Kye said, "You can let go of me, now. They can't see us from here, and I can walk the rest of the way."

Cara looked at Kye questioningly.

"It's not sprained," Kye said giggling. "Look, I can walk perfectly."

Cara was shocked. Kye had faked it to get out of running! Cara couldn't believe it. She never did anything to get into trouble. *Quinn* was the one who was always getting detention, not Cara. She wanted to ask Kye why she'd faked it, but Cara knew that Kye wouldn't think she was cool if she said something about it.

"What was your name?" Kye asked. "Cara?"

"Right," Cara said. "Cara Knowles. And you're Kye Baldwin?"

"Yup, the one and only," Kye kidded.

"Did you live in New York City?" Cara asked, her blue eyes glowing with admiration.

"Yeah, the Big Apple," Kye said. "We lived on Park Avenue. It was kind of dead. But I hung out in the Village a lot. That was very."

"Oh, the Village," Cara echoed, trying to sound as if she knew what Kye was talking about. What Village? And it was very what? "That sounds totally awesome!"

"It was," Kye admitted. "Nothing like Florida. Palm Beach is really bogus. What do you guys do down here, anyway?"

"Well, we have a lot of parties," Cara said, a little hurt by Kye's attitude. "In fact, I'm having a big party this Friday. Why don't you come?"

If Cara was expecting Kye to jump at the chance, she was disappointed. "A party, huh?" was all Kye said.

"Yeah, it should be pretty wild," Cara said. "Everybody's going!"

14

"Even that goody-goody, Lynn or whatever her name is?"

"Oh, no!" Cara exclaimed, shocked. "I would never invite *her*."

"Well, I don't know."

"There'll be a lot of seventh graders there, too," Cara boasted.

"And guys?" Kye asked. "I haven't met any guys here, yet. Don't you hang out with boys here?"

"Of course we do," Cara said indignantly. "And of course there'll be boys at the party. Sixth *and* seventh graders."

"Well, maybe," Kye said ungraciously. "I'll think about it. Hey, let's get a soda from the machine and hang out in the locker room until class is over," she suggested.

What if Ms. Bosson checks with the nurse? Cara thought immediately. But "okay" was all she said.

Back on the track, the girls were finishing up their laps.

"Where'd Cara go?" Stephanie asked Patty as she caught up to her. Patty was running with Jesse and Mimi.

"I think she took Kye to the nurse," Patty offered.

"Doesn't she usually run with you?" Stephanie asked Jesse. "What was she doing with Kye today?"

"How should I know?" Jesse exclaimed angrily. "I can't read her mind. She can do whatever she wants!" Jesse had been Cara's best friend for as long as she could remember. They did everything together. And being Cara's best friend meant instant popularity, and Jesse loved

15

that even if Cara always had to be the boss. Jesse couldn't understand why she felt so left out all of a sudden. Just because Cara felt like running with someone new shouldn't be such a big deal. But it was. And why did everybody have to notice when Cara didn't run with her?

"Sor-ry," Stephanie said huffily. "I was just asking. You don't have to get all bent out of shape about it." With that she sped up and joined Quinn and Esme, who were running about twenty yards in front of Jesse.

"What's up, guys?" Stephanie greeted them. Even though she was one of Cara's crowd, she and Quinn were pretty friendly. Ever since soccer season, when they won the State Championship and tied the G. Adams boys' team, Quinn and Stephanie hung out together sometimes. Cara wasn't very happy about it, but Stephanie was the most independent of Cara's friends and she basically did what she wanted. She was always telling Quinn that there was more to Cara than met the eye. But sometimes even Stephanie wasn't so sure.

"Hey, Steph!" Quinn said. "How goes it?"

"Okay," she answered. "Jesse's mad at me though. Well, she's probably more mad at Cara for running with that Kye girl. What's with that girl, anyway?"

"She's not very friendly," Esme said. "In English class she called Quinn a goody-goody and a teacher's pet."

Stephanie had to stop running because she was laughing so hard. "Quinn's . . . a . . . teacher's . . . pet?" she stuttered between gasps.

"C'mon, Steph," Quinn urged, jogging in place.

16

"You know it's true. I really am a goody-goody. I've never gotten into any kind of trouble at PBP. I am *the* model student," she finished. She couldn't say this with a straight face, though, and soon she joined Stephanie, laughing hysterically at the thought.

"Guys," Esme began, "you're causing a scene. I mean, it's funny and all, but not *that* funny."

Stephanie and Quinn tried to compose themselves. "Sorry, Es," Quinn apologized. "We'll try to behave in a more decorous manner."

"Fine," Esme agreed, even though she had no idea what "decorous" meant.

At that moment, Ms. Bosson blew her whistle. "All right, girls!" she screamed. "That's enough for today! Stretch for a few minutes, and then you can all head inside!"

The girls stretched, and then Quinn jumped up. "I'd better hurry!" she exclaimed. "I don't want to be late for social studies. I have to make sure I get that seat in front, and I want to go over an extra credit project with Ms. Gordon before class starts, and . . ." Quinn couldn't finish her sentence, she was so overcome with laughter.

"C'mon you teacher's pet," Stephanie challenged, "I'll race you back to the gym!"

Esme, Quinn, and Stephanie ran back to the gym, laughing the entire way.

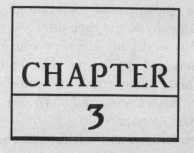

CHAPTER 3

"So what are we going to do on Friday night?" Esme asked Quinn and Alicia that afternoon. "Since we haven't been invited to the biggest social event of the year."

"I'm sure we'll think of something," Quinn said. "Why is this party such a big deal anyway?" The three of them were at Scoops, the local ice cream parlor. Nicole had riding practice that afternoon, so she wasn't with them. Esme had insisted that she couldn't make it all the way home unless she had a banana split. Esme was eating a gigantic one with extra hot fudge sauce, and Quinn and Alicia were sharing one. They couldn't understand how model-thin Esme could eat so much and never gain an ounce. Quinn called her "Hoover" because of the way she inhaled food.

"*Caramba*, Quinn," Alicia answered. "There are going to be a ton of *boys* there—older boys—boys in Jonathan's class. How can you even ask that?''

Quinn looked embarrassed at the sound of Jonathan's name. She kind of liked Nicole's stepbrother, Jonathan Stanton. He was in seventh grade at G. Adams, and he kind of liked her back. But she didn't want to talk about it with her friends, especially Nicole. It was kind of an awkward situation. And she would die before she let them know how she felt about him.

"Well," Alicia continued, "why don't we have a sleepover at my apartment? We can rent a movie or something."

"Rent a movie?" Esme asked nervously. "What *kind* of movie?"

"I was thinking maybe *Hellraiser*," Alicia suggested.

"What!!" Quinn and Esme exclaimed together.

"Isn't that the movie with that guy who has pins stuck all over his face?" Quinn asked.

"Yeah, Pinhead," Alicia answered. Alicia loved horror movies. She had seen all of the *Friday the 13th* and the *Nightmare on Elm Street* movies, and she was always trying to get her friends to watch them with her. Quinn was usually the only one who would. Nicole found them disgusting—all that hacking—and Esme couldn't watch an entire film. She usually ended up with her face in a pillow so she didn't have to see any of the scary scenes.

"What?" Alicia asked, finally noticing her friends' silence. "Don't you want to see that one?"

19

"Well, Lish," Quinn began, trying to be tactful. "We might enjoy seeing something else more."

"Like what?" Alicia asked, slightly hurt that her friends didn't share her love of horror.

"Well, I wanted to see that movie with Corey Haim and Corey Feldman where they learn to drive, and . . ." Esme began.

Quinn noticed the look of distaste on Alicia's face. Alicia couldn't stand the teen flicks that Esme went crazy over. Quinn was pretty flexible, and would watch just about anything.

"What about something like *Lost Boys*?" Quinn asked, trying to avoid a fight. "I heard that's supposed to be really good, and Corey Haim and Corey Feldman are both in it. And there are supposed to be some really scary scenes."

They had finally agreed when Nicole arrived. "Practice was over early," she said. "They're doing something to the ring to get it ready for the show next week."

Nicole ordered a chocolate milkshake, and listened to the three of them make plans for Friday night. She wished that she had never been invited to Cara's stupid party. It wouldn't be any fun without her friends.

"So, what do you guys think about that new girl?" Alicia asked, through a mouthful of ice cream. "She's got a major attitude."

"*Really,*" Quinn agreed. "And the worst of it is that Mr. Holmes wants me to help her catch up in English— as in after-school studying."

"That's terrible," Nicole sympathized.

"Yeah," Esme agreed. "And you guys will never believe what Kye thinks of Quinn . . ." She paused dramatically for effect. Esme loved to pause dramatically, even though it drove her friends crazy.

"What, Hoov?" Alicia asked impatiently.

Esme pretended to pout. Quinn answered instead. "She thinks I'm a teacher's pet and a brown-noser."

Alicia snorted, then laughed. But her mouth was full of melted ice cream, and when she laughed, it came out her nose.

"Oh, gross!" Esme exclaimed, laughing.

"That's totally disgusting, Lish," Nicole admonished.

"Well, it's not like I did it on purpose," Alicia said, defending herself, as she wiped the ice cream off her face. "That is really funny about Kye, though. But if she doesn't like goody-goodies, why is she hanging out with Cara?"

"The Queen of the Brown-Nosers?" Quinn asked. "Beats me."

"Patty Porter was in the office dropping off the attendance sheets and heard that Kye had been kicked out of a few schools in New York before she came down here," Nicole said.

"You're always finding things out," Quinn teased. "Why don't any of the rest of us hear what you hear?"

"I heard that, too, Quinn," Esme said. "And Patty said that she overheard Mrs. Hartman talking to Ms. Bauer who said that Kye's father sent her down here to live with her aunt—who just *happens* to be a good friend of Heartburn's."

21

"Now, that's some real dirt, *chica*!" Alicia exclaimed.

"That's just gossip," Quinn said. "You never really know with Patty."

"That's true, you have to take everything she says with a grain of salt," Nicole added. "All I know is that in math today, Kye didn't even seem to know what a fraction was. She doesn't seem the type who studies either. You've got your work cut out for you, Quinn."

"Really," Alicia agreed. "You just better hope that you don't have to help her out in every subject."

Kye was the subject of another conversation that afternoon. Cara and her friends were squeezed into a booth, sharing a large cheese pie at Pizzarama.

"Yeah, Heartburn said that her mother died a long time ago," Patty finished. She took a long drink of her diet soda. Cara was always ordering diet drinks for them. Patty hated the taste, but she supposed Cara was right—she could stand to lose a few pounds.

"So, she really is nothing but trouble," Jesse said, relieved. Maybe Cara would stop being so interested in Kye now.

"That's not *true*!" Cara exclaimed. "She's really cool. I like her. She's so New York, and she hung out in the Village and all." Cara still had no idea what "Village" Kye was talking about, but she liked the way it sounded. Besides, she'd never let her friends know that she had no clue what this place was.

"So?" Stephanie asked. "She's really not very

friendly.'' She giggled. ''And you know what Quinn told me today?'' Cara's eyes narrowed a little at the mention of Quinn, but she didn't say anything. ''Kye thinks Quinn's a goody-two-shoes!''

Patty and Mimi laughed. Cara turned and gave them a look, and they both shut up abruptly. And Jesse had a feeling that Cara was not about to leave Kye alone.

''Quinn is a bit of a teacher's pet,'' Cara said. ''Don't you notice the way she acts with Mr. Holmes? She totally brown-noses him!''

Patty and Stephanie looked at each other in confusion. Quinn was anything but a teacher's pet!

''That's ridiculous, Cara,'' Stephanie contradicted her.

''Shut up, Barnyard!'' Cara yelled. ''She is too, and that's that. Kye thinks so, too.''

''So what if she does?'' Patty muttered under her breath.

''What?'' Cara asked.

''Nothing,'' Patty answered, looking into her soda glass.

''Anyway, I invited her to my party,'' Cara announced a few moments later.

''You did what!'' Jesse exclaimed. ''This is a very exclusive party, Cara. I thought only the right people were invited. You can't just invite Kye—you don't know the first thing about her!''

''Of course I do!'' Cara retorted. ''I told you she's really cool, and it's my party after all.''

''Fine,'' Jesse said, picking up a piece of pizza. She didn't want Cara to see how upset she was. It was only

23

a stupid party. She shouldn't be so hurt. "But that doesn't mean *I* have to be friends with her!" Jesse threw her pizza back down on the tray and stood up. She looked as if she wanted to say something else to Cara, but then thought better of it and stormed out of Pizzarama.

"What's wrong with *her*?" Cara asked. Everybody suddenly got very busy with their pizza or their sodas, and no one answered her. She didn't seem to notice. "Anyway, Kye is really wild. She told me that she saw a Tom Cruise movie being filmed last month right outside her building, and she even went over to meet him. She got his autograph and everything!"

The other girls all rolled their eyes and didn't say anything. Stephanie and Patty turned most of their attention to their food, and Mimi tried to look a little interested in hearing all about Kye.

"And *Ghostbusters II* was filmed right down the block from her, and she went down every day after school to see it," Cara went on.

"And she saw Tom Selleck and his baby in FAO Schwartz all the time, and . . ."

The next half hour dragged on and on, with Cara telling the other three all about Kye—more than they ever wanted to know. Cara told them about how Kye had gotten kicked out of two schools in New York. Of course it had only been because they had these really stupid rules, so it wasn't like it was her fault or anything.

Finally, Stephanie stood up and said she had to get going. Patty jumped up and followed her out. Mimi was trying to think of a way to leave too, when Cara herself

decided she had to get home. She had given Kye her
phone number and Cara hoped she'd call. Cara was definitely in the mood for someone new. Kye wasn't at all
like any of her other friends, and Cara was really glad
she had moved to Palm Beach—no matter what anybody
else said.

117231

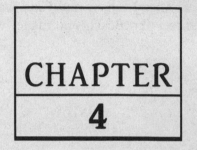

CHAPTER
4

"Uh, oh," Cara whispered to Kye the next afternoon at lunch. "Heartburn's at the end of the line checking uniforms."

Every once in a while, Mrs. Hartman would show up at lunch period and stand at the end of the food line. She checked every girl to make sure she was in uniform. Heartburn confiscated any article of clothing or jewelry that was against the rules, and the student had to pay her a quarter to get it back at the end of the day. She had sent more than one girl to the bathroom to wash off excess makeup, and had welcomed them back to the cafeteria with a detention slip.

"So what?" Kye retorted. "What's she going to do?"

"Kye, you're not in uniform!" Cara said. Kye was wearing a white T-shirt under her uniform jacket with THE SUGARCUBES written on it. Cara had asked her about it, and Kye had said that they were a band from

Iceland. She acted as if she couldn't believe that Cara had never heard of them. Cara had vowed never to ask her about anything like that again. She definitely wanted Kye to think she was cool, too. Also, Kye's jacket was covered with buttons and pins. To say nothing of her bright orange lycra tights.

Kye acted quite calm as they got closer and closer to Mrs. Hartman. She placed her lunch on a tray, and was reaching for milk when Mrs. Hartman finally spoke.

"Miss Baldwin," Mrs. Hartman said. "You are not in proper uniform. This *should* mean a detention."

Kye knew she was home free then. Heartburn didn't say she *was* going to get detention. She just said that it *should mean* detention.

"I'm sorry, Mrs. Hartman," Kye apologized in a sickly sweet voice. "I didn't have time to get any white blouses yet. I promise that I'll try to buy one after school today."

"Okay, Kye," Mrs. Hartman said. "Since you're new, I will only give you a warning. But take all those buttons off your jacket; and Kye, we don't wear hats indoors."

Kye was wearing a black, almost brimless hat, which she had pulled all the way down on her head. Her forehead was totally covered, and her eyes barely showed. Cara thought it was really wild—she had never seen anything like it before. Of course, Kye had gotten it in the Village. Cara really wanted to see what this Village was like. It sounded immense.

Even after they sat down, Kye didn't make any move

to take any of her buttons off, and she left her hat on. Cara couldn't believe that she was disobeying Heartburn, especially when the headmistress was still in the cafeteria. But Cara knew better than to say anything.

Kye had refused to sit with the rest of Cara's friends. She told Cara that they weren't nearly as cool as she was, and she couldn't understand what Cara saw in them anyway. "Cara, you're really much better off without them. They're so conservative. I don't know how you can hang out with them," she had told her earlier.

"So, are you going to come to my party?" Cara asked, as she took a bite of her spaghetti. The sauce looked and tasted like Campbell's tomato soup. "Did you ask your aunt?"

"I don't have to ask her anything!" Kye retorted. "I can do whatever I want!" She attacked her own spaghetti. "I haven't decided what I'm doing on Saturday yet," she continued obnoxiously. "If nothing better comes up, I guess I'll go."

Cara felt hurt, but didn't want to show it. "Well, I don't know what I'm wearing yet. I have to get something really wild."

Kye snorted. "Something wild?" she asked sarcastically. "In Palm Beach? Please."

"The Palm Beach Mall has a new store. It's from New York—the Unique Boutique," Cara said, trying to make Palm Beach sound a little cooler.

"Unique?" Kye asked in surprise. "Unique is in Palm Beach? The store in the Village is so wild. I'd love to check it out."

28

"I'll go with you," Cara said. "Maybe one day after school?"

"Maybe," Kye agreed.

Two tables down, Alicia was talking very quickly as she gestured in Cara's direction. "You should have seen her this morning in French class," she said. "Monsieur Delacroix actually yelled at Cara for whispering in class to Kye."

"Cara got yelled at?" Nicole asked. "I don't believe it! All the teachers love her."

"Well, she got caught daydreaming in science," Esme informed them. "You should have seen her face when she realized that a whole class was staring at her, waiting for her to answer the question she hadn't even heard!"

A few tables away, Jesse was sitting with Stephanie, Patty, and Mimi. She was not happy that Cara was not sitting with them.

"Is she too good for us now?" Stephanie asked, gesturing at Cara.

"I heard she cut school for a whole *month* in New York," Patty said, inclining her head towards Kye.

"Really?" Mimi asked.

"Don't you think that's a bit ridiculous, Patty?" Stephanie said. "Someone would have noticed, don't you think?"

"I think *she's* ridiculous," Jesse said suddenly. "What is she wearing that hat for—it's almost seventy degrees out!"

"She could have done it," Patty retorted, turning to Stephanie. She hated it when someone doubted her in-

29

formation. They didn't call her the Mouth for nothing. "If she showed up for morning attendance, checked in, and then left, no one had to know. All schools can't be as strict as PBP, you know! And I heard the ones in New York are a lot less structured."

"Well, whether it's true or not," Stephanie said, trying to appease Patty, "I don't really get what Cara sees in her. She's not all that great."

"I don't either!" Jesse exclaimed. "I mean just because she's from New York City and all. I think she's trouble!"

Right after lunch, the entire school had an assembly. Some college students from the S.A.M.S. (Students Against Multiple Sclerosis) fundraising committee were coming to talk to the girls to see if they could get some support at PBP.

Everybody was jammed into the auditorium when Alicia, Nicole, Esme, and Quinn finally got there. They couldn't find four seats together and had to go down to the front row in order to sit together.

"Next time try to fix your hair a little faster, Es," Quinn reprimanded.

They ran down to the front row, and slid into the first four seats just as Mrs. Hartman stood up to call the school to order.

Mrs. Hartman started to introduce the visiting college students when there was a loud snapping sound from the audience. Mrs. Hartman paused, and peered over the top of her half-glasses. All the girls looked attentive. Quinn turned around, and spotted Kye cracking her gum—loudly. But every time the headmistress looked up, Kye was just sitting there, looking as if she was seriously concentrating on the assembly.

Finally, the college students got up to speak. Their talk was very interesting. They told the girls what Multiple Sclerosis was, and what was being done to discover a cure for it. The S.A.M.S. speakers made it clear to the girls that as PBP students, even they could really do something to help.

After the assembly, before her friends could say anything, Alicia walked up to one of the S.A.M.S. people and started talking to him. He called Mrs. Hartman over, she listened for a minute, and then patted Alicia on the back.

"What's going on up there?" Nicole asked Quinn and Esme, who were waiting for Alicia in the aisle of the auditorium. By now most of the other college students were gathered around Alicia, who was smiling broadly.

Finally Alicia rejoined them, and they headed up the aisle.

"What was *that* all about?" Quinn asked Alicia.

"Well, I thought, I mean as president of the sixth grade, I thought that *we*, the sixth grade at PBP, should *do* something for S.A.M.S. I think it's such a great organization, and to actually be able to help . . ." Alicia's voice trailed off.

"That's great!" Nicole exclaimed.

"I love the idea that *we* can do something!" Quinn added.

31

"I know," Alicia agreed. "I thought that we could raise some money for S.A.M.S."

"What would we do?" Esme asked.

"I suggested a car wash, and everybody else loved the idea," Alicia answered. "Even Heartburn."

"Can we get G. Adams to help us out?" Esme asked excitedly. "That would be really, really cool!"

The other three laughed. "That's true," Alicia agreed. "I'll have to give Peter a call tonight."

"Calling Peter, are you?" Quinn teased. Peter Zermatt was the president of the sixth grade at G. Adams. He and Alicia had to work with each other a lot to plan all the events the two schools did together. And there were a lot of joint events since G. Adams was PBP's brother school. All her friends teased Alicia about Peter, even though she insisted that she really liked Tyler Stein.

"Well, I'm sure you wouldn't mind running into Jamie Farber again at the car wash," Alicia accused.

Quinn felt her face get warm, and Alicia thought that she had hit a nerve. But Quinn was not blushing because she liked Jamie. The truth was that she hadn't even thought about him in ages. Ever since the Sadie Hawkins Dance, Quinn had only thought about one guy—Jonathan. Nicole's stepbrother had even kissed her that night, but none of her friends knew anything about it.

Luckily, the bell rang and Quinn was spared from further teasing. The girls had to run to get to their next classes before they were really late.

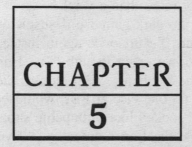

CHAPTER 5

"Psst!" Cara hissed, pointing to the note on Jesse's desk.

Jesse glanced down at the little rectangle of looseleaf paper and realized that this note was not meant for her at all. It was for Kye, who was sitting in the next row, on Jesse's right.

Jesse looked furious as she tried to discreetly slip the note to Kye. She had no intention of getting caught passing notes from Cara, her supposed "best friend," to this new girl. Kye, meanwhile, was so deep in her own thoughts that Jesse had to whisper her name twice to get her attention.

Jesse was angry, and it wasn't just that Ms. Gordon might turn around at any moment. She was writing notes on the blackboard about the Louisiana Purchase or something equally uninteresting to her sixth grade history class. Jesse was upset because she was dying to know what Cara's note to Kye said. She was hurt that Cara hadn't let her in on it. After all, she had been Cara's best friend since kindergarten. Kye had scarcely been at Palm Beach Prep for more than a week.

Jesse eyed the dark-haired girl suspiciously. She was wearing a white T-shirt once again instead of the regulation button-down, even though Mrs. Hartman had had a fit about it the day before. Her clunky black shoes were so weird that no one else at PBP would be caught dead in them. They looked like orthopedic shoes.

From almost the first moment that Kye had arrived, Cara had spent almost all of her time with her. It made Jesse feel very unsure about where she stood in her own friendship with Cara. She looked back at Kye.

The other girl was looking at the clock impatiently, anxious for the class to end. She was concentrating on how she could cut her last class without getting caught. After a minute or two, she picked up the note that Jesse had given her. Without even trying to hide it from Ms. Gordon's view, Kye unfolded the piece of paper. It said, "Kye, want to check out Unique after school today?—Cara."

That was *exactly* what Kye had in mind. But she had no intention of waiting until *after* school. Plus, she had a foolproof plan about how to get out. She wrote back, "I'm blowing off math class and leaving next period. You can come if you want."

Jesse gave Kye a killer look as the note to Cara hit her desk. Kye smiled obnoxiously at Jesse and went back to thinking about her plan.

34

Cara carefully unfolded the note and read it. She really wanted to go to that new store today, but she *couldn't* go with Kye. Cutting school was just too much. She had never cut school in her life. Yet she really *wanted* to go. She didn't want Kye to think she wasn't cool. But what was she going to tell her? She didn't want to look like a total wuss by not cutting. She'd have to think of a great reason why she couldn't go. Cara nibbled on her eraser, then ripped out a clean sheet of paper. She thought for a minute before she began to write.

Everyone in the class jumped as the familiar crackling noise of the loudspeaker sounded. The voice of Mrs. Hartman came across loud and clear.

"Attention!" the headmistress announced. *"Would Miss Quinn McNair please report to the office immediately? Thank you."*

"What now?" Quinn muttered as she gathered up her books. She gave the loudspeaker an annoyed glance. "Just once, I'd like to get through a day without seeing Flo's office. I spend more time there than she does . . ."

Kye swivelled in her seat to look at Quinn in surprise. She couldn't imagine what in the world Quinn was muttering about. Wasn't Quinn a goody-goody? What would *she* be called to the office for?

Quinn picked up her stuff and headed for the door. "I'm really sorry, Ms. Gordon," she apologized.

"That's all right, Quinn," the history teacher reassured her. "You can stop by my office later to see what you missed in class. Good luck."

After Quinn had left, Kye glanced at the clock impa-

35

tiently, anxious for the class to end. She had a great plan. The lower school had recently been hit with a stomach virus, and everyone was afraid that it would spread all over PBP. That virus was just the ticket she needed to get out.

The bell finally rang for the end of class, and Kye went straight to the nurse's office. She didn't even wait to talk to Cara. If Cara didn't want to go that was fine with her. She would just go by herself.

At the nurse's office, she told the nurse that she felt sick to her stomach and she couldn't finish her lunch. The nurse stuck a thermometer in her mouth and walked out of the room. Kye jumped up and put the thermometer on a lightbulb, keeping an eye on the reading to make sure the temperature didn't get too high. Spotting a wet washcloth, she picked it up and rubbed her forehead.

The nurse came back in, just as Kye sat back down and stuck the thermometer in her mouth. "Oh, you're a bit warm here, dear," the nurse said, clucking her tongue. She reached out her hand to feel Kye's forehead. "You feel kind of clammy, too."

Half an hour later, Kye was walking through the mall. She laughed to herself—these people were such pushovers. It was a lot harder to convince the nurses in New York. Not that she never succeeded. She'd gotten out of classes quite a few times. Kye thought the schools totally overreacted those few times they had caught her. It was no big deal. And it wasn't like her father was all broken up about it. He just shipped her off to his aunt in Palm Beach. It made her feel like a piece of luggage.

Kye continued to walk through the mall until she found the Unique Boutique. It was just like the one in New York, right down to the plaster of paris people on the ceiling, and it had exactly what she wanted to wear to Cara's party. The black lacy miniskirt would be perfect with a short white top. She wanted to look very New York. She *was* planning on going to the party, but she didn't want anyone to be too sure of her actions. Kye liked to be mysterious and to keep people on their toes, so she never let anyone know what she was doing until the last minute.

She dug her father's credit card out of her wallet. He had told her to use it only in case of emergency. This was definitely an emergency. Living in New York her whole life, Kye's warm weather wardrobe was severely limited. Anyway, she was bored and needed to buy some new things.

The minute Kye got out of the store, she headed for the mall bathroom to change out of her uniform. She pulled on a pair of long white cuffed denim shorts and a cropped black T-shirt, wadded her uniform up into a ball, and shoved it into her bag.

When school officially let out for the day, Alicia, Nicole, Esme, and Quinn rode their bikes over to the mall. They were browsing through some of the clothes in Mrs. Antona's boutique, which were very pretty and expensive, too.

"Nicole, I think you should get something *new* for this

party,'' Esme said. She was over at the counter trying on all the scarves.

"Yeah," Alicia agreed. "You never know *who* might be there. I think you need to get a new outfit."

"Come on, guys," Nicole complained. "I don't need anything new. I have plenty of clothes at home. I'm sure I'll find *something* to wear."

"You shouldn't just wear *anything*, Nicole," Quinn contradicted. "You'd probably go in your uniform if you couldn't find anything else."

Out of the four girls, Nicole was the only one still in uniform. The others had changed as soon as they had gotten out of school. Nicole really didn't care about clothes. If it was comfortable and practical, she'd wear it. She spent a lot of time in either her school uniform, riding jodhpurs, or jeans. Her friends were always trying to get her to buy some new clothes.

"I would not!" Nicole exclaimed. "Give me a little credit, Quinn. I'm not about to wear my uniform to a party."

"Right," Quinn agreed. "So let's get you something a little outrageous, eh?"

"I don't know about that, Quinn," Nicole said hesitantly.

"I think that's a great idea!" Esme agreed enthusiastically.

"Let's go to that new store," Alicia suggested. "My mom told me they have some really wild clothes."

"Well, you don't have to ask me twice," Esme joked.

"But can we get something to eat afterwards? I'm starved."

"What's new?" Quinn teased.

"*Adios*, mama!" Alicia said as she kissed her mother good-bye. "See you later!"

"Bye, Mrs. Antona," the other three girls called us Alicia dragged them out of the store.

It took them half an hour to reach the new store. They were sidetracked in the record store, where they checked out all the new releases and Quinn bought the latest *Rolling Stone* magazine. Then they had to stop in the bookstore to see Esme's new spread in *Seventeen*. After the bookstore, they made it as far as the drugstore. Esme had quite a few beauty products to purchase—hand cream, body cream, face cream, a specific kind of soap, and special shampoo. Alicia got stuck in the nail polish aisle for ten minutes before deciding to buy this weird red-pink color called "Cherries in the Snow."

Finally they reached Unique. None of them had ever seen anything like it. There was an old-fashioned bench out front with plaster of paris people sitting on it. Everything in the window was neon-bright, and the sign was splatter-painted. "This is really wild!" Quinn exclaimed. "Let's go in!"

"Guys," Nicole objected, trying to turn them away. "I really don't think this is my kind of store. *I* would never find anything to wear in there. Why don't I just meet you guys somewhere else?"

"Come on," Esme urged, practically dragging Nicole

into the store. "I know we're going to find just the thing for you!"

The store was jammed with funky clothes. There was an entire section just for hats, and there were all these upside-down plaster of paris people stuck on the ceiling. Quinn walked around for a while, craning her neck, checking it all out.

"Hey, these are way cool," Quinn said, holding up a pair of huge drawstring khaki pants.

"Sure, Quinn," Esme agreed. "You can wear them on your next safari." She picked up a denim jacket with a sequined pattern of the New York skyline on the back. "This is wild, eh?" she asked the others.

"This is it!" Alicia exclaimed, holding up a black rubber dress with zippers everywhere. "This is what Nicole should wear to Cara's party!"

Nicole looked a little nervous until she realized Alicia was joking.

"Now, these would cause Flo a little heartburn, don't you think?" Quinn asked, holding up a pair of multi-colored neon socks with silver peace signs all over them. "Maybe I should get a pair," she added, her blue eyes twinkling.

"Don't you have enough pairs of crazy socks?" Esme asked, shaking her head. She couldn't understand Quinn's thing for socks.

"You can never have enough!" Quinn exclaimed.

"Come on, guys," Alicia instructed. "We have to find something for Nicole to wear."

Nicole spent the next forty-five minutes getting in and

out of the craziest outfits. First, Alicia picked out a leop-
ard print jumpsuit, then a neon green lycra dress, and
then a pair of ripped-up blue jeans with tights underneath
and a white undershirt. After that, she chose a pair of
orange stretch pants with a black cropped top, a shapeless
batik print dress, a black shirt with a zipper neck and
black lycra capri pants, and finally the black rubber dress.

Nicole was exhausted and starving after the ordeal,
and they still hadn't found anything.

"How about this?" Quinn asked, holding up a royal
blue sleeveless mini-dress with matching capri-length
leggings.

"That's cool," Esme said. "You'd look great in that,
Nicole."

"Try it on," Alicia instructed.

Nicole sighed, but knew that they were not going to
leave the store until she had bought something. Besides,
this outfit was not nearly as wild as some of the other
stuff they had made her try on. Nicole slipped into it and
pulled the dress down over the leggings. She couldn't
believe it, but she actually kind of liked it.

"Well?" an impatient voice came from outside the
dressing room. "Can we see it?"

Nicole stepped out, and her friends "oohed" and
"aahed."

"That's perfect!" Esme declared.

"I really like it," Quinn echoed.

"Of course you like it, you chose it," Alicia teased.
"But really, Nicole, it looks great on you."

"I think you should buy it," Esme said, more like a command than a suggestion.

Nicole couldn't agree more. She was starving, and the only way they'd agree to go get something to eat would be for her to buy something. And who knows? She might actually wear the outfit.

Quinn decided to buy the peace sign socks. She got into line behind Nicole and Esme, who had needed no urging to get the denim jacket with the Manhattan skyline across the back. Alicia was debating over T-shirts. She couldn't decide what color to get. Quinn almost fell over backwards when she saw what Esme and Nicole had spent on their purchases. Quinn was just not used to the way people in Palm Beach spent money. She was from a middle-class family in Nueva Beach, and for two towns so close, the lifestyles were completely different.

After Alicia had bought a fuchsia shirt, they all headed over to the food court.

"Hey, isn't that Kye?" Nicole asked, pointing across the mall as they headed up the escalators.

"Well, let's not go out of our way to say hello," Alicia said. "She would probably just ignore us anyway."

"I can't believe her!" Quinn exclaimed.

"What are you talking about?" Esme asked, pulling her new jacket out of the bag to admire it.

"After I got out of Heartburn's office, I saw her signing out of school with a note from the nurse saying she was sick. She doesn't look too sick now," Quinn observed.

"Well, you know, it doesn't surprise me," Alicia said,

stepping off the escalator and heading towards the food court. "After what Nicole and Esme heard from Patty, I'm sure she cuts school a lot."

"You know she's going to Cara's party, don't you?" Nicole asked, grabbing a table.

"What?" Esme, Alicia, and Quinn exclaimed.

"I'm sorry, Nicole," Quinn apologized.

"What for?"

"This party is really going to be *fun*," Quinn said sarcastically. "And we talked you into it."

"Who knows?" Nicole asked. "My mother would probably have made me go anyway. And I don't have to stay that long. Besides, who's going to tell you all about it, if not me?"

"Okay, okay," Quinn said laughing. "But I'm still sorry about it."

"Hey, can we eat now?" Esme asked impatiently.

"Stop drooling, Es," Alicia reprimanded. "Go get food. We'll meet you back here."

All thoughts of Kye left their minds after they got their food and started planning the S.A.M.S. car wash.

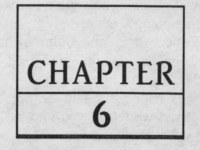

CHAPTER
6

"**S**o, what time are you leaving for the party?" Esme asked Nicole on Friday afternoon.

"Well, it starts at seven," Nicole said reluctantly. "I really don't want to go without you guys."

"Nicole," Quinn scolded, "you *are* going to have a good time tonight, and then you're going to tell us all about it tomorrow!"

The four girls were on their way to Nicole's after school. They rode up Nicole's driveway and parked their bikes, then started walking around the back of the house.

"What are you guys doing tonight, anyway?" Nicole asked, opening the back door.

"We're going over to Alicia's to see some movies," Esme said. "Maybe we'll even get around to doing a few of those posters for S.A.M.S."

Nicole looked as if she felt totally left out, so they hurried to reassure her that they would miss her.

"Hey, Nicole, don't worry," Quinn said. "We'll be sure to leave you a few posters to do."

"Yeah, and we'll definitely miss you during the movie," Esme said with a shudder. "Lish, of course, is renting some horror movie."

"It's not *really* a horror movie," Alicia retorted defensively. "Those Corey actors you like so much are in it, and the sound track is great."

"All right, all right," Esme whined. "Can we get something to eat now? I'm starved."

Her friends laughed. "Of course you are," Quinn said. "You're a Hoover."

"Cut it out, Quinn," Esme replied. "I am not!"

"I'm just joking. You sure get grouchy when you're hungry!"

They all raced into the kitchen. Quinn opened the door and ran smack into Jonathan. He was wearing his longish brown hair in a ponytail, and had a gold hoop in his left ear. Quinn took in his ripped Levis and white T-shirt, and wished she had changed out of her uniform.

"Slow down, Quinn," he said, laughing. "Do you want to kill me or something?" He grabbed her shoulders to stop laughing. Quinn hadn't really talked to Jonathan that much since the Sadie Hawkins Dance. Almost every time he saw her he reminded her that she still owed him a pizza. Quinn didn't know how she'd explain to Nicole about a date with her stepbrother. It was a very confusing situation.

"Hi," Quinn managed to say before Alicia, Nicole, and Esme came barreling into the kitchen behind her.

45

Nicole stopped short at the sight of Jonathan. "Oh, hi," she said flatly. "Mom said you were going to Cara's party tonight."

Quinn looked startled. Jonathan was invited to this party, too?

"Yeah," he answered, looking at Quinn. "Are you going?" he asked her.

"Oh, no!" Quinn exclaimed. "I'm not *cool* enough to be invited. Cara will probably never allow me in her house again."

"Again?" he asked. "I'm sure there's a story to this."

Nicole looked from Quinn to Jonathan and back to Quinn. "So, how are you getting there?" Nicole asked him.

"Adrian and I are going over together," he said, picking up the carton of milk on the counter and heading for the door. "Sorry you won't be there, Quinn," he called over his shoulder before the door swung shut behind him.

Quinn's friends turned to look at her. Quinn suddenly became very busy looking in the refrigerator for soda. "What kind of soda does everybody want?" she asked, hoping to shift their attention back to food.

"Nicole," Alicia said, "you must be pretty desperate to ask Jonathan how he's getting there. You *really* don't want to go to this party, do you?"

Nicole sighed. "Not really," she admitted. "And I kind of hoped I could go over with someone—even Jonathan."

"Come on, Nicole," Alicia said. "I know you're going to have fun. Let's go get you ready for the party."

"What do you mean, get me ready?" she asked nervously.

"Well," Esme began, "we've got to do your hair, your face, make sure you wear the right shoes with your new clothes . . ."

Nicole wailed. "This is so stupid! What am I doing this for?"

"It'll be great!" Alicia exclaimed. "Let's go up to your room to get started."

Half an hour later, Nicole was sitting on a chair in her room wearing her bathrobe, her hair dripping wet, surrounded by Esme, Alicia, and Quinn.

"Do you really think that's necessary?" Nicole asked, eyeing the Hot Sticks Esme had just plugged in. "I mean, we'll be swimming and all."

"But you want to look good when you make your entrance, don't you?" Esme asked. "First impressions are so important."

Nicole really wanted to see what they were doing to her, but she wasn't allowed to look in the mirror. They worked on her for what felt like hours. Finally, they let her get dressed. Esme and Quinn dug around in her closet looking for shoes, while Alicia kept her away from the mirror.

At last, Nicole was allowed to take a peek at herself. She was in total shock.

"Oh, my gosh," was all she could say. Nicole's straight brown hair, which was usually pulled back into a ponytail, was curled and hung loose to her shoulders.

47

And she looked fantastic in her new outfit. "Is this really me?" Nicole gasped.

"Wow!" Esme exclaimed. "You look great!"

"Really!" Quinn concurred.

"I can't believe it!" was all Alicia could say.

"So, are you ready to knock Knowles-It-All off her feet?" Quinn asked. "You are going to be such a hit!"

It was time for Esme, Alicia, and Quinn to get going. They had to pack for their slumber party, and Alicia had to pick up the video. Nicole was sorry to see them go, but she was getting kind of excited about this party—a little bit anyway.

At seven-fifteen Nicole walked around the back of the Knowles' estate. All the lights along their palm-lined driveway were on, and there were lanterns strung between the trees. The grounds were perfectly manicured, as usual, and the hibiscus bushes, which were in full bloom, gave off a sweet smell. Music was blaring out of four large speakers at the corners of the patio. The pool and patio were already crowded with kids. Nicole couldn't believe how many people were there.

"Nicole!" someone called. Nicole looked around and spotted Virginia Choy calling her from a table by the pool. "Over here!"

Gratefully, Nicole headed over to the pool.

"Hey," a voice behind her said. Nicole whirled around and found herself face to face with Dana. He stared at her for a moment. "You look different!" he finally exclaimed.

Nicole blushed. She had almost forgotten about her

new look. Maybe it was all a big mistake. She wished she could go back to the way she was before. Dana was staring at her as if she were from another planet or something. She turned to go. He pulled her back and turned her around.

"No, I mean, you look great!" he corrected. He stared at her until she squirmed under his gaze.

"Thanks," she murmured. Nicole didn't know where to look or what else to say. Boys were so much harder to deal with than horses. Why had she come to this party, anyway?

Dana looked as if he wanted to ask her something, but just then three of his friends came up behind him and dragged him off. He gave Nicole an apologetic look as he left, and winked broadly at her. "I'll talk to you later," he called just before he was thrown into the pool.

Nicole tried to avoid the splashes, and finally plopped down in a chair opposite Virginia.

"Nicole, you look incredible!" Missy exclaimed.

"Really," Virginia agreed. "You should wear your hair down more often."

"Look!" Missy ordered, pointing. Kye had just walked in, her timing perfect to make just the entrance she wanted. She was wearing the little lacy black miniskirt and cropped white shirt. She had on her clunky black shoes with white socks. Kye hadn't met any of the G. Adams boys before, so Cara was making sure that she met them all now. They were hanging all over her. Kye made her way to some empty lounge chairs near the girls' table, and Cara and a crew of boys followed.

Missy, Virginia, and Nicole watched as a bunch of boys gathered around Kye's chair and fought each other for the right to get her a soda.

"So, you're from New York, eh?" Adrian asked Kye. "That's really cool. My friend Jonathan's from Manhattan, too."

Nicole couldn't believe it when Jonathan joined Kye's group of admirers. She was really glad, though, when Dana walked right by Kye without a backwards glance. He jumped back into the pool.

The guys in the pool wanted to start a big water volleyball game, and tried to talk some girls into it, too. Virginia and Missy dragged Nicole inside to change into their suits. Kye said she definitely didn't want to go swimming. Of course, the group of boys around her said they didn't want to go either.

Nicole, Virginia, and Missy ran into Stephanie and Patty inside.

"Hey, guys," Stephanie greeted them. "How's it going?"

"We had to leave the patio," Missy complained. "The hormone club out there was getting to us."

"And the Kye Baldwin fan club," Virginia added, heading up the stairs to change. Patty and Stephanie followed.

"I can't believe how Cara's following Kye around like a sick puppy," Patty said. "*She* always has to be the center of attention, but now she doesn't seem to care if Kye gets it all."

"I know," Stephanie agreed. "It's really weird. And

Jesse is so mad, she could spit. I've never seen her like this before."

"Well, Cara *is* ignoring all of us," Patty said.

"We're obviously not good enough for her anymore," Stephanie added. "Only those seventh graders are cool enough for her to hang out with. Hey, who cares? Who needs her anyway?"

After they had changed, the five girls hurried back downstairs. As Missy had said, they didn't "want to miss out on jumping into a pool full of gorgeous guys."

Soon everybody who wasn't part of "Kye's fan club" was in the pool playing volleyball.

Finally, Dora, Cara's maid, came down to the patio and called everyone out of the pool. Dinner was ready. A twelve-foot-long buffet table was covered with barbecued ribs, chicken wings in spicy sauce, chips, dip, and salads.

Virginia, Missy, and Nicole pulled large T-shirts over their wet bathing suits and sat down to eat. They had each taken a few bites when Missy looked up and started to giggle. "Virginia, your face is covered with barbecue sauce!" she exclaimed.

Virginia retorted, "Well, so is yours!" Then they both looked at Nicole and started laughing even harder.

"Nicole . . . your nose!" gasped Virginia, pointing to the sauce on the end of Nicole's nose.

"Oh, no!" Nicole cried, reaching for her napkin. It was totally covered in sauce already, though, so she stood up to get another.

Before she had gone a few steps away from the table,

Dana appeared in front of her. "Need a little help?" he asked, as he wiped the sauce off her face.

Nicole froze. "Hey," Dana said softly. He reached up to touch her wet hair, but stopped right before he did. "You looked great when you got here, but I like you a lot better this way, Nicole," he said seriously. This only made Nicole more flustered. Dana was never serious. What was with him now?

Nicole heard Virginia and Missy laughing. She didn't know where to look. Dana cleared his throat nervously. Nicole raised her eyes, and found him staring down at her. "I have to get a napkin," she said softly, moving around Dana. She looked back at him when she reached the table, and he was still standing there.

After everyone had finished eating, Cara led them all into the living room for some movies.

"This is *so* boring!" Kye whispered loudly when the movie was half over, even though Cara was sitting right next to her.

"We could put on another movie," Cara suggested quickly. "We have a ton to choose from."

"It's not *that*," Kye continued, without lowering her voice. "It's just that these guys are such babies, and your girlfriends are *total* snobs."

Cara didn't know what to do. She hoped her friends hadn't heard what Kye had just said. What if they thought her party was a complete flop? She had to think of some way to make Kye happy.

"I know," Kye exclaimed suddenly, standing up. "Let's go to the beach."

"The *beach*? What for?" Cara asked, looking upset. It was dark out, and she definitely wasn't allowed to go to the beach at night. Her parents would ground her for life.

"Look over there," Kye replied, pointing to a small flickering light a short way down the beach. "I heard that some freshmen from G. Adams were having a cook-out. Now *that* sounds like fun!"

"I don't know," Cara said, hesitating.

"Oh, come on, Cara," Kye nagged. "Or are you a baby, too?"

Great, thought Cara. If I don't go, she'll think I'm a wimp, but if I do, I may get into major trouble. She looked over at Jesse and Mimi, who were staring at her, waiting to see what she would do.

"Well, are we going or what?" Kye said, interrupting Cara's thoughts.

"Uh, I guess if it's close," Cara said, trying to sound enthusiastic. "Who else wants to go down to the beach?"

No one looked as if they were about to move. Anne Marie and Virginia shook their heads, and Mimi and Jesse looked away.

"Come on, Cara," Kye said. "Let's blow this pop stand."

"We'll be back soon," Cara told her friends. She definitely felt weird about leaving her own party, and she was nervous about going to a high school beach party. Reluctantly, she followed Kye out of the room.

"Let's sneak out the back door," Cara whispered to Kye. "If we get caught, we're really in trouble."

"Hang on," Kye said, pausing at the window by the door. She undid her long braid, and let her hair flow in waves down her back. Then she reached into her pocket and pulled out some red lipstick. "Want to wear some?" she asked Cara. Kye looked so *old*! She took the lipstick from Kye and put on as little as she could. Then she followed Kye out the door, and they both headed for the point of light about a quarter mile down the beach.

The closer they got to the bonfire, the more nervous Cara became. She looked around at all the older kids, and felt really uncomfortable about being there. "Kye," she whispered. "We don't know *anybody* here. Maybe we should go back!"

"Oh, come on! Don't be such a goody-goody," Kye snapped. She stalked away from Cara, and was quickly surrounded by a couple of good-looking guys.

Cara stood there shivering. Nervously, she pulled her oversized letter jacket tightly around her. What am I doing here, she thought. And how am I going to get back into the house without getting caught? Her friends were definitely going to be angry with her, and if her parents found out, she'd really get it. She watched Kye flirting with a tall, blond guy, and suddenly she felt sick. Just then, there was a flash of lightning and it started to drizzle. People began to gather up their things quickly to leave.

"Kye," Cara called. "Will you hurry up?"

"Chill out," Kye yelled back. "I'll be there in a minute."

Cara took off her jacket and used it to cover her head.

She watched as Kye said good-bye to the blond guy, and walked slowly back towards her. Maybe we'll make it home without getting too wet, Cara thought. But just as Kye reached her, there was another flash of lightning, quickly followed by a loud clap of thunder, and before Cara could say anything, it began to pour.

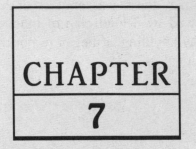

CHAPTER
7

"**I**s it morning already?" Esme groaned, as she stretched her legs out to the bottom of Alicia's couch and pulled a pillow over her eyes.

"Es," Quinn exclaimed, "it's almost eleven o'clock! You *can't* be tired. You've had at least ten hours sleep!"

"That movie Alicia made us watch gave me nightmares! I was awake half the night," Esme murmured sleepily. Alicia had rented *The Lost Boys*, and Esme had spent a lot of the movie lying facedown covering her ears.

"You mean you kept dreaming that Keifer Sutherland was coming to bite your neck," Quinn teased in her best Dracula voice.

"Don't *remind* me of that," Esme commanded. "I don't want to hear anything else about it!"

The phone started to ring, and Esme put her hands back over her ears. Alicia picked it up and said, "Vampire residence." There was a short pause. Then Alicia exclaimed, "Nicole, oh my gosh, we've been waiting for you to call!"

"Ask what happened, ask what happened!" Esme screamed as she bolted up into a sitting position on the couch. She suddenly looked wide awake.

"Find out about the party," Quinn said.

Alicia motioned to her friends to be quiet so she could hear. "We're just trying to drag Esme out of bed," she told Nicole. "Are you back from riding already?"

There was a murmur on the other end of the line. "She just got back," Alicia translated. "Nicole wants us to come over for lunch. Then she'll tell us what happened."

"We'll be right there!" Alicia assured Nicole before she hung up the phone.

"Did she say anything?" Quinn asked.

"She'll tell us everything when we get there," Alicia said.

"I can't wait," Esme exclaimed. "Let's go!"

"Cornflake, you're not even dressed yet!" Quinn said.

"I'll be ready in two minutes," Esme promised, giggling.

"That'll be the day," Quinn teased. "It'll be two *hours* if we're lucky."

"Quinn!" Esme yelled, pretending to be upset. Then she threw her pillow in Quinn's direction and ran into the bathroom to change. About fifteen minutes later, she was actually ready. Quinn and Alicia couldn't believe it. It was definitely record time.

The three girls sped over to Nicole's and knocked

57

loudly on the front door. They could hear Nicole thumping down the stairs yelling, "I'll get it."

"Good," Jonathan called out from the kitchen. "It's probably for you, anyway."

Nicole ignored him and opened the door. "Hi, guys," she said, as Alicia, Quinn, and Esme tried to control their excitement.

Nicole followed Esme, Alicia, and Quinn upstairs to her room and shut her bedroom door.

"So what happened?" the three girls yelled as soon as the door was closed.

"You'll never believe it," Nicole began, sitting down on her bed. "I don't even know where to begin."

"Tell us *everything*!" Esme exclaimed.

"Well, first of all, Cara spent the entire evening with Kye," Nicole said. "She ate with her, and she didn't even swim because Kye didn't want to." Nicole stopped for breath, while Esme looked at Alicia in amazement.

"What did Jesse and those guys do?" Esme asked.

"Yeah, who else was there?" added Alicia.

"Wait," Nicole said. "This is the best part. We were in the middle of watching a movie when Kye started complaining. She said she thought that all the guys at the party were babies. Can you believe it?"

"That's terrible!" Esme screeched. "How dare she call Bobby a baby! So what did Cara do?"

"Well, Kye told Cara she wanted to go to a beach party some G. Adams High School guys were having!"

"No way!" Quinn exclaimed. That was a bit much, even for her.

"Oh my gosh! I can't believe it!" Esme screamed. "Did anyone go?"

Nicole nodded.

"Who?" Alicia asked.

"Cara went with Kye, of course," Nicole began. "No one else wanted to go, so Kye and Cara snuck out. They stayed there a little while and then that thunderstorm started. Dora caught them trying to sneak in, totally drenched!" Nicole finished.

"Did Cara get in a lot of trouble?" Quinn asked. She couldn't believe that goody-goody Knowles-It-All would do something like that.

"I don't know. Cara went running upstairs to change and Jesse went after her. Then we heard Cara yelling at Jesse to get out of her room and leave her alone. Jesse was so upset she called her mother right away to come and get her. About half the people had left by the time Cara came down to say good-bye."

"That must have been really embarrassing in front of all those guys!" Esme commented. "I wonder what Cara's parents will do."

"Do you think they'll ground her?" Alicia wondered out loud.

"I don't know," Nicole answered, looking serious. "The guys thought the whole thing was really funny. They couldn't believe Kye and Cara actually wanted to sneak off to a high school party."

"Which guys were there, anyway?" Esme asked, trying to sound casual.

"Oh, I don't know," Nicole said, shrugging. "Bobby was there, of course, and so was Tyler."

"You're so lucky," Alicia groaned. "I would do *anything* to go to a party with Tyler."

"I didn't go with him," Nicole corrected. "He was just there."

"Who else?" Esme asked eagerly. "Which seventh graders?"

"I don't really remember. You know Jonathan went, and Adrian, and Dana—"

"*Dana* was there?" Esme asked teasing. "Did you talk to him?"

Nicole blushed. "A little," she confessed, but she definitely didn't want to tell them how he had told her she looked really good.

"Earth to Nicole," Esme interrupted Nicole's daydreams. "Can we eat lunch soon? I'm starved."

"What a surprise," teased Alicia.

The girls spent the afternoon by the pool, and then Alicia suggested they go to Scoops.

"I can't," Quinn admitted. "I have to go home."

"Why?" Alicia asked. "I thought we were going to work on the S.A.M.S. posters tonight."

"I have to study with Kye. Actually, I'd better get going. I have to meet her at my house in about half an hour."

"Why are you studying with *her*?" Esme asked.

"I told you," Quinn replied. "Mr. Holmes wants me to be her study partner until she's caught up on her work and everything."

"On a Saturday night?" Alicia exclaimed.

"It was the only time *she* had free," Quinn said sarcastically. "Believe me, I'm not exactly thrilled with the arrangement."

"So why don't you blow her off and come out with us?" Esme asked, a devilish grin on her face.

"Because of Mr. Holmes, Es," Quinn retorted. "I promised, you know."

"And we all know how you feel about him . . ." Alicia teased.

Quinn blushed. "Look, kids," she said. "I can't help it if you guys are always drooling over him."

"Quinn's blushing," Esme pointed out. "I mean, totally blushing."

"I think this is my cue to exit," Quinn replied dramatically. "I'll call you later. Bye."

With that, she was off. The other girls looked at each other and shrugged. At least *they* didn't have to spend the evening with Kye.

"Quinn, some girl is here to see you!" Patrick yelled from the bottom of the stairs. He looked like a miniature Quinn, with the same red hair and big blue eyes. He was short for his age, but his loud mouth certainly made his presence known.

"Tell her to come up," Quinn screamed from her room. She was trying to get ready to tutor Kye. The last thing she wanted to be doing on a Saturday night was schoolwork.

"Hey," Kye said, as she walked into Quinn's room without knocking.

"Hi," Quinn replied coldly. "Well, let's get started," she suggested. The sooner they began, the sooner they'd be finished. Maybe she could still hook up with her friends after all.

Kye didn't make any attempt to begin. She looked around Quinn's room instead.

"You know," she suddenly said. "There are no cool places to go around here. That's probably why you guys don't do anything but study all the time. I never asked for a study partner, you know."

"Look," Quinn said, clenching her teeth in anger, "I can think of better ways to spend my Saturday nights, too. But Mr. Holmes asked me to do this and I really had no choice. So let's get some work done, okay?"

Kye looked at Quinn for a moment. "Okay," she finally muttered after an awkward pause.

"So, where are your books?" Quinn asked.

"At school," Kye said flippantly. "I forgot I might need them this weekend."

"No problem," Quinn said, trying to swallow her anger. "You can just use mine. I'll give you some paper and a pencil too."

"I have a better idea," Kye replied, with a trace of a smile on her face. "I'll study with you, but do we have to study tonight? Let's wait till Monday after school."

"So why did you make me cancel my plans and then come all the way over here before telling me?" Quinn exclaimed. "You have a telephone, don't you?"

Quinn watched the smile fade from Kye's face. Suddenly she began to feel a little sorry for her. She remembered how it was to be a new student in a strange school, with most people suspicious of you. It wasn't easy, especially in the middle of the year.

"I'm sorry, Quinn," Kye apologized. She said it awkwardly. It certainly didn't sound as if Kye apologized all that often.

"Well, as long as we're definitely starting Monday," Quinn said, relenting. "Maybe I can still get ahold of my friends."

Kye stood by while Quinn called Nicole, Esme, and Alicia, but none of them were home. And no one had a clue where they were. Quinn figured they were at Scoops or Pizzarama or something, but she couldn't be sure.

"Great," she muttered. "Now I'm stuck at home on a Saturday night."

"There's a pretty decent band playing nearby," Kye mentioned, taking Quinn by surprise. "Why don't we go check it out?"

"We'd never get into a club!" Quinn exclaimed, without thinking.

"Sure we will," Kye retorted. "I did things like this all the time in New York. It'll be fun."

Quinn hesitated for a minute. She didn't exactly like Kye, but then she had never tried to sneak into a club before, and she thought it might be fun. She was always up for trying new things. And anything was better than sitting home. "Why not?" she said. "Let's go." Besides, this sounded like a pretty cool adventure. Quinn

63

thought for a moment. "Hey, wait a minute," she said. "I have a great idea. My brother, Sean, is in a band— why don't we take a few pieces of his equipment and try to get in through the back door? If they stop us we'll just say that we're with the band."

"Not bad!" Kye exclaimed.

Sean had already gone out for the night, but Quinn didn't think he'd mind if they borrowed a few things. She had hung out with the band for long enough to know which equipment she could touch without him minding. She took two microphone stands and told her parents that she and Kye were going for a walk, and then over to Palmetto Pete's. She didn't consider this a lie because she didn't believe that they would really get into the club. She figured that they'd end up at Pete's, and that trying to get into the club was more like a detour.

"Okay," she said to Kye. "Let's go!"

About half an hour later, the two girls walked into Palmetto Pete's. Quinn was laughing so hard that she could hardly talk.

"Oh my gosh, I can't believe we did that!" Quinn cried.

"That was so funny!" Kye exclaimed, giggling. "That guy with the long hair looked exactly like Axl Rose! He was such a jerk!"

"I can't believe he didn't believe we were with the band," Quinn said. "Who would carry around microphone stands for fun?"

"Maybe it would have worked better if the stage manager hadn't been standing right there," Kye added. As she looked over at Quinn, both girls started laughing again. Quinn was really surprised, but she had to admit she was having a good time. She couldn't imagine Alicia, Nicole, or Esme trying something like what they'd just done.

"Hey, this place isn't so bad," Kye said, interrupting Quinn's thoughts.

"Yeah, I hang out here a lot," Quinn replied. "You should have some french fries—they're great. Oh, and have a milkshake."

"How about onion rings?" Kye added. "I'm ready for a feast. I missed dinner tonight."

"You don't have to eat with your aunt?" Quinn asked.

"I can do whatever I want," Kye snapped.

There was an awkward silence. What was with this girl? Quinn had just asked a simple question. She wondered why Kye had been so defensive. To keep the peace, Quinn changed the subject.

"Did you have fun at Cara's party?" she asked.

"Are you kidding?" Kye exclaimed, smiling again. "You are so lucky you didn't come. I mean it was so boring, I almost fell asleep. Cara's friends are such snobs."

Quinn thought it was weird that Kye thought Cara's *friends* were snobs, but not Cara. Cara was more snobby than her friends. Yet Kye didn't seem too stuck-up.

Kye didn't like Quinn's friends either. Every time Quinn mentioned them, Kye would roll her eyes and change the subject. Earlier in the evening, Kye had actually asked Quinn why she hung out with them. She said something about Quinn being too cool for them. Quinn had angrily defended her friends, but Kye quickly changed the subject again. She was definitely difficult to figure out.

CHAPTER
8

"Those two make me sick," Esme muttered the next morning, as she watched Cara and Kye walking into the cafeteria together. "They deserve each other."

"Kye told me that she thought all of Cara's friends were snobs," Quinn explained to her friends.

"And she doesn't think Cara is?" Alicia asked. "Miss Knowles-It-All is the queen of snobs."

"I know," Quinn agreed. "I really don't get it."

"Well, Kye must be as big a snob as Cara is, then," Alicia commented.

"Come on, Lish," Quinn said, suddenly feeling kind of angry. "You don't know her. She wasn't snobby on Saturday night." Quinn thought her friends were unfair not to at least give Kye a chance. They had given Quinn a chance when she had first come to PBP—in fact they were the only ones who had. Why was Kye different? It wasn't her fault if she wasn't like the other girls at PBP.

Quinn knew how that felt only too well. Being different wasn't easy.

"Are you guys coming over this afternoon to study for the history quiz?" Nicole asked, changing the subject.

"I'll take all the help I can get," Esme groaned.

"Of course," Alicia added.

"I can't—" Quinn began.

"Why not?" Nicole asked. "I thought we decided last week to get together today."

"We did," Quinn agreed. "And I'm sorry, but I have to study with Kye."

"Well, why don't you bring her along?" Esme asked. "She has to take that quiz tomorrow, doesn't she?"

"That's a good idea, Es," Nicole agreed. "And then you guys can finish your other subjects later," she said to Quinn.

A few tables away, Kye sat close to Cara, unaware that her afternoon was being planned for her.

"This place is such a drag," Kye complained. "School is a total waste of time. Why don't we get out of here?"

"You mean, you want to finish lunch outside?" Cara asked.

"I didn't mean *that*," Kye said, laughing. "I meant leave-leave. You know, take a half day."

"Cut school?" Cara exclaimed, trying not to sound too shocked.

"Look at it out there," Kye commanded. "It's beautiful. If I have to be stuck down here in Florida, the least I can do is get a decent tan."

68

"I don't know," Cara said hesitantly. "I don't really think we should."

"Oh, come on, Car," Kye pleaded. "It'll only be fun if you come with me."

Cara thought about it for a minute. Kye really wanted her to go, and it did sound like fun. Besides, none of her other friends would ever dream of cutting school. And Cara loved to be the first one to do things.

"How will we leave without getting caught?" Cara asked, trying not to sound as nervous as she felt.

"We'll just sneak out the back door," Kye said. "Come on, this is going to be great!"

"Won't the teachers notice we're gone?" Cara asked, a little shakily. What was she getting herself into? Kye didn't give her a chance to worry any further, though. When she made up her mind to do something, it was impossible to say no.

"What's the worst thing that could happen?" Kye went on. "Mrs. Hartman *might* call your parents and have a little chat. You're already grounded. What else can they do to you?"

"That's true," Cara agreed. "I guess I can only be grounded once." Kye looked at her and smiled broadly, and Cara felt pretty good. The whole idea of cutting school was actually kind of exciting.

"All right, let's go," Cara continued, as she and Kye got up from their table. They walked out of the cafeteria, and up to their lockers to dump their books. Then they ran down the hall to hide in the bathroom until the late bell rang and the hallways cleared.

The two girls had almost made it to the back door when they almost ran smack into Mrs. Hartman. Cara gasped. Kye nudged her in the ribs.

"Miss Knowles, Miss Baldwin, aren't you supposed to be in class now?" Mrs. Hartman began, looking over the tops of her glasses at them.

"We . . . we . . ." Cara stuttered.

"Cara had a terrible stomachache after lunch," Kye cut in quickly. Cara couldn't believe how fast she answered. And Kye didn't sound nervous or anything. "I thought I should take her to the nurse." She paused dramatically. "I really thought she was going to be sick— her face was a horrible shade of green a minute ago."

Mrs. Hartman furrowed her brow in concern.

"You do look a little pale, dear," she said to Cara. "I'll take you to the nurse myself. Kye, you may go back to class."

Kye flashed Cara a grin, winked broadly, and turned to walk back to class.

Cara's heart was racing as she walked into the nurse's office. She couldn't believe she had almost cut school, not to mention almost getting caught by Mrs. Hartman. Jesse and Mimi would die! She was surprised that the nurse and Mrs. Hartman couldn't hear her heart pounding. She was so nervous that her palms were sweating. She was actually beginning to feel sick. She clutched her stomach tightly, and sat down on the bed.

"Is there anything else I can do for you?" Mrs. Hartman asked, concerned.

"Uh, n-no, thank you," Cara stuttered. "I'll be all right in a little while."

"She probably has the stomach virus that's been going around," the nurse told Mrs. Hartman. "I think I'll send her home just to be on the safe side."

Cara started to say that she'd be fine, but then stopped herself. After all, an afternoon off was what she had wanted in the first place.

"Shall I call your mother?" the nurse asked.

"I don't think she's home," Cara said. "But I'm sure the housekeeper would be able to pick me up." As she lay down on the bed, waiting for Dora to arrive, she imagined what the rest of her afternoon would be like, by the pool, in the sun, listening to music, maybe even swimming. And she would miss the Latin quiz. Suddenly, cutting school didn't seem like such a bad idea at all.

Later that afternoon, five girls sat in Nicole's room, studying. Actually, four of them were studying—Kye was just sitting there, staring out the window. "Well, what do you think, Kye?" Nicole prodded.

"What?" Kye asked blankly. Alicia was getting pretty angry. This had been going on for forty-five minutes already, and Kye was making absolutely no effort to do any work.

Nicole, however, was all patience. "Why do you think Jefferson made the Louisiana Purchase?" she asked Kye again.

"How should I know?" Kye retorted. "I really could care less why Jefferson bought anything."

Quinn was beginning to wonder why she had ever felt sorry for Kye. Kye was no help at all in their studying. In fact, she was slowing everyone down. And she was anything but friendly. "Well, maybe you should care. You want to pass, don't you?"

Kye looked at Quinn. "Maybe," she replied sullenly.

"Well, then why are you here?" Esme asked bluntly. Tact was not Esme's strong point. Besides, she really wanted to know. She thought she was bad. Kye was ten times worse. She didn't know a thing. And she didn't care.

"I really couldn't tell you." Kye answered obnoxiously. "I wish we hadn't gotten caught cutting today, then I wouldn't be here at all."

"What are you talking about?" Quinn asked, her eyes narrowing.

Kye shook her hair back. "Cara and I tried to cut out of school today, but Heartburn caught us." She laughed. "It was really kind of funny. And then we had to pretend that Cara was sick and I was taking her to the nurse. So Cara, that rat, got to spend the afternoon by the pool, and here I am, studying."

Quinn couldn't believe this girl. Now she was cutting school. And getting Cara to cut with her. Quinn wondered if Cara really knew what she was getting herself into. "You think that's cool, cutting school?" she asked Kye. Her friends looked at Quinn in surprise. Quinn was speaking in a tight, almost strangled voice that they knew meant she was trying to keep her temper.

"Sure," Kye said flippantly. "You don't? Don't be so uptight, Quinn."

Alicia, Nicole, and Esme looked from Quinn to Kye and back to Quinn. Sparks were practically flying out of Quinn's ears. However, all Quinn said was, "I've had enough studying. I've got to go." She packed up her books and turned to Nicole, Alicia, and Esme. "I'll talk to you guys later," she said. Then Quinn turned to Kye. "Give me a call when you're ready to study." Then she was gone.

After she left, Kye looked at the three unfriendly faces around her. "Well, I'm blowing this pop stand, too," she stated. She gathered up her unopened books and threw an "It's been fun," over her shoulder on her way out.

"That girl is *loco*!" Alicia exclaimed after Kye had left.

"Yeah, really!" Esme agreed.

"She's obviously driving Quinn crazy," Nicole commented. "It sounded as if she and Kye had a pretty good time on Saturday night. But I don't think Quinn likes her anymore."

"Well, I don't like her at all," Alicia added. "She's totally rude."

"Why did Quinn ever think Kye might be nice?" Esme wondered, as the three of them returned to their studying.

CHAPTER
9

"Hey, Quinn, wait up!" Kye yelled on the way to lunch the following day.

Quinn turned around and stopped. "What?" she asked shortly.

"I wondered if you wanted to study tonight," Kye said, flashing Quinn a smile.

Quinn thought Kye had a lot of nerve to be acting so nicely to her. She really did not want to study with Kye anymore, and was about to tell her so. But then she remembered her promise to Mr. Holmes.

"Fine," Quinn practically spat out. "You can come over after school."

"Great. I'll meet you at your locker," Kye said, and ran off, leaving an angry Quinn behind.

Quinn ran to catch up to Alicia and Esme, who had already started walking down the hall to the cafeteria. She couldn't help wondering about Kye. She changed personalities the way some people changed their socks. Quinn definitely could not figure her out. Actually, she didn't even want to try.

Quinn, Esme, and Alicia got their food, and walked over to a table to sit down.

"What did Kye want?" Alicia asked as Quinn took a seat.

Quinn opened her milk and picked up a straw. "She wants to study tonight." Angrily, Quinn pulled the wrapper off the straw. "Can you believe it?"

"I'd believe anything that girl does," Nicole replied. "She spells trouble."

Esme nodded vigorously in agreement.

"I know you promised Mr. Holmes," Nicole continued, "but there are limits. I mean, she's got to want to work."

"I know, I know," Quinn agreed in a weary voice. "I'm going to give her one last chance. And then, that's it."

"That's more than I'd give her," Alicia said, taking a savage bite out of her tuna melt. "Why you are so nice to her is beyond me."

"It's beyond me, too," Quinn replied.

After school, Kye was waiting by Quinn's locker.

"You ready?" she called out as Quinn came down the hall.

"Yeah, let me grab my books," Quinn replied, trying to keep an even tone. Didn't Kye realize how mad Quinn had gotten yesterday?

"Hey, Kye, where are you going?" Cara asked, coming down the hall from the other direction.

"I'm going over to Quinn's," she replied, turning back to Quinn. "All set?"

"Quinn's?" Cara asked questioningly. Cara thought that Kye thought Quinn was a real goody-goody. What would she be going over there for? And then Cara remembered that Mr. Holmes had asked Quinn to help Kye catch up. "Oh, to do homework?" Cara asked, sneering.

Quinn felt the hair on the back of her neck stand up on end. It always did that when she was angry. And Cara Knowles-It-All always made her angry.

"Actually, we're going to watch my brother's band rehearsal," Quinn cut in. "You remember *Sean*, don't you?" she couldn't help adding, wondering why she had said anything. She remembered how Cara had thought Sean was really cute when she first saw him. When Alicia ran for class president against Cara, Sean's band, the Nueva Beat, had played for Alicia's pre-election party. Cara had been staring at Sean during the whole performance. But when Cara found out that he was Quinn's brother, she had run out of the room.

But why Quinn felt she had to say anything at all to Cara was a mystery. She *really* was going to just study with Kye. She didn't want to do anything else with her. But there was something about the way that Cara thought she knew everything and tried to control everyone that got Quinn mad.

Cara was at a loss for words for a moment. Then she noticed that Kye didn't seem to know anything about a band rehearsal. Quinn was definitely up to something. Knowing that, Cara smiled, and told Kye she'd talk to her later.

"That sounds like fun, Quinn," Kye said excitedly on their way out. Quinn could have kicked herself as she and Kye walked towards their bikes. Now the afternoon was going to be endless. Why did she have to open her big mouth?

"I didn't know your brother rehearsed at your house," Kye said as she and Quinn were riding over to Nueva Beach. "That's pretty cool. Why didn't you tell me sooner?"

"I don't know," Quinn admitted. As much as Quinn disliked Kye, she wasn't about to tell her that she had only used her to get back at Cara. In fact, she was almost ashamed to admit it to herself. "I don't listen to them all the time."

They could already hear the pulsing reggae beat as they parked their bikes in Quinn's driveway. "They sound pretty good," Kye said. "Almost as good as some of the bands in New York."

Quinn waved to Sean as they walked into the living room. They plopped down on the couch and watched the band. The guys started really hamming it up. Quinn knew that the Nueva Beat loved an audience and couldn't help performing for them.

After about forty-five minutes, the band stopped. Quinn clapped and whistled as Sean took off his guitar. "That's it, guys," he announced.

"You guys aren't too bad," Kye said almost obnoxiously, as if she were some kind of record producer or something.

"Well, thanks," Ricky, the drummer, replied.

"Uh, guys," Quinn broke in hurriedly. "This is Kye Baldwin. I'm tutoring her for school. She just moved here from New York." Quinn wanted to make sure that they knew that Kye wasn't really her friend. She couldn't believe that Kye had just acted so obnoxiously.

Kye got up and started walking around the living room while the band packed up their equipment. "I mean, I've heard better in New York," she continued, "but you definitely have potential."

Sean raised his eyebrows at Quinn, who shrugged. Ricky looked as if he wanted to bash Kye over the head with Sean's guitar.

"You guys should go up to New York," Kye continued, oblivious to everyone else's growing anger. "You can't expect to be able to do anything stuck down here in Florida. Unless you're not really serious about this."

"Thanks for the advice, *chica*," Ricky said, emphasizing *chica* in a not very friendly way. "Your opinion is very important to us."

Kye looked surprised that anyone would speak to her like that. "Hey, I'm only trying to help," she said, backing up toward Quinn. "Forget I said anything. Rot in Florida—see if I care."

Sean shot a "get her out of here" glance at Quinn. Ricky had an incredible temper and Sean could see it was on the verge of exploding.

Just then, Patrick came racing into the room.

78

"Hey, it's Patrick!" Sean screamed. He jumped up from the couch, grabbed his little brother, and started swinging him around the room.

"Stop!" Patrick screamed, between giggles.

"Sean!" Quinn yelled, even more loudly. "You're going to knock something over, and then you'll really be in trouble."

"Attack!" commanded Sean, as he and Patrick raced over and pounced on Quinn. The three of them collapsed on the floor as Kye stood there, watching.

"Woaahh!" Quinn exclaimed as Patrick narrowly missed hitting his head on the coffee table. "Cease fire."

"I have to get to work, anyway," Sean said. He had a job as a sales clerk in a music store in Nueva Beach.

"Yeah, we've got to go study," Kye added. "Let's go, Quinn," she practically ordered.

Quinn looked helplessly at Sean, and picked up her fallen book bag. "See you later, guys," she called out as she trudged up the stairs, Kye following right behind her.

"I wish my room at my aunt's looked like this," Kye said, as soon as they reached Quinn's room. Quinn had posters of UB40, INXS, Ziggy Marley, and U2 hanging on her walls. She also had her entire button collection pinned to a bulletin board.

Quinn fidgeted in her chair. How Kye could act as if she hadn't just acted like a total jerk to Sean's band was beyond Quinn. She had better get Kye caught up quickly, so she would go home sooner. "Let's do the math problems," Quinn said, opening up her notebook.

"All right, all right," Kye agreed, much to Quinn's surprise. "What chapter are we on?"

"Chapter seven," Quinn replied, trying to clear her mind. "We have to do word problems one through fifteen."

"One through fifteen!" Kye exclaimed. "That could take all night."

"Just do your best," Quinn said, hoping that it wouldn't take that long. She couldn't wait to get rid of Kye. "We'll work on them for a half an hour, and then compare our answers. They're not that bad."

Quinn got to work. The homework really wasn't hard because it was a review of the work they had been doing for a couple of weeks.

About twenty-five minutes later she had finished. "How are you doing?" she asked Kye.

"I hate math," Kye answered, quickly covering her work.

"I'm going down to the kitchen to set the table. I'll be right back," Quinn said, leaving her math homework on top of her book. "I'll check out your answers when I get back." She hoped Kye would be finished by the time she got back.

"Cool," Kye said, shrugging her shoulders.

When Quinn got back to her room, Kye was leaning over Quinn's math homework, writing quickly. "What are you doing?" Quinn asked quietly. Quinn quiet was always much more dangerous than Quinn yelling.

Kye jumped back. "I was just checking my work," she said. "I couldn't do any more so I thought I'd check the ones I had done. You said we were going to check them over, so what's the big deal?''

"You should do it all yourself," Quinn said, not really knowing whether or not to believe Kye. She walked over to the desk. Kye tried to hide her paper, but Quinn grabbed it. Kye had only tried to do two of the problems, and she had copied the rest from Quinn.

"It doesn't look like you're just checking!" Quinn accused her.

"What are you getting so worked up about, Quinn?" Kye asked, shrugging her shoulders and grabbing her paper back. "It's not like I killed anyone or anything. It's only some stupid math homework."

"Yeah," Quinn retorted, trying to stay calm. "But I didn't say you could copy from me."

"Fine," Kye spat out. "You're just like I thought. You're such a goody-goody! Cara was right!" She grabbed her bag and stormed out the door.

That girl has some serious problems, Quinn thought, and turned back to her desk to finish her homework. The day I'm a goody-goody, she mused laughing. I've probably been called into Heartburn's office every other day on the average. Goody-goody—yeah, right! Kye was one mixed-up girl and she definitely had it all wrong.

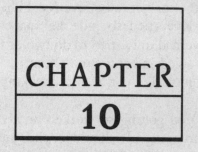

CHAPTER
10

"Jesse!" Cara called out across the PBP parking lot. "Wait up! Didn't you hear me?"

"No," Jesse lied. She had seen Cara parking her bike, but she'd decided to walk straight towards school instead. She couldn't face being ignored again when Kye showed up.

"Let's go over the science homework," Cara commanded. Jesse found it very difficult to say no. She always said yes to Cara. She also missed hanging out with Cara. "Kye is *so* bad in science," Cara continued. "It's not worth it to compare answers with her."

"I don't have mine with me," Jesse told Cara.

"Well, let's go get it," Cara suggested. "Jess, we always check homework answers."

"Not lately," Jesse answered, hurt. Then, as she saw Kye ride up on her shiny red bike, added, "There's Kye, Cara. Aren't you going to go talk to her?"

"Come on, Jess. What's with you?" Cara asked, walking up the front steps with Jesse.

"Nothing," Jesse muttered. "I just don't think that you have to forget all about your old friends, just because you have new ones."

"Pul-lease," Cara whined. "I'm not ignoring you. You just don't seem to want to hang out with Kye. You don't like her anyway."

"I never said that!" Jesse retorted. "You just never invite me anywhere with you."

Well, that was because Kye thought Jesse was totally uncool, Cara thought. She had to admit that she thought Jesse was out of it sometimes, too. Cara didn't really want to share Kye with anyone either. She liked the fact that Kye thought *she* was totally cool, and she'd hate for Jesse to spoil that image. But Cara felt sort of badly about Jesse. She missed her. And hanging out with Kye was kind of exhausting. She always felt as if she had to prove something.

"Well," Cara said slowly. "We're going to the beach tomorrow. You can come if you want." One afternoon wouldn't kill her.

Jesse was shocked. "You want *me* to go to the beach with you and Kye?" she asked in surprise.

"Yeah, sure," Cara replied quickly. What was she getting herself into?

The next morning, Jesse was pacing up and down the sidewalk near the beach entrance. "She's twenty minutes late," she complained to Cara. "Are you sure we were supposed to meet her here?"

83

"She'll be here," Cara snapped, looking up and down the street. She knew this had been a bad idea. Kye hadn't been too happy when she'd found out that Jesse was going with them.

Finally, five minutes later, Kye appeared, riding slowly down the street. She cruised to a stop in front of Cara and Jesse.

"Hey, guys," she said, shaking her head in an exaggerated motion so that the girls would notice her hair. She had pulled it up into a high ponytail and braided it into at least thirty very thin braids. Then she had tied the bottom of each with a different colored ribbon.

"That looks great!" Cara complimented, picking up on the not-so-subtle hint. Jesse noticed that Cara didn't even mention the fact that they had been waiting for almost half an hour for Kye to show up.

Cara looked at Jesse meaningfully and nudged her.

"Yeah," Jesse added, "it's really cool."

"Thanks, Car," Kye said, ignoring Jesse's compliment. "Let's hit the beach. Don't want to miss peak tanning hours, do we?" The three of them locked up their bikes and walked quickly across the hot sand, searching for the perfect place to lay out their towels. Jesse spread hers out carefully, securing the ends with her sneakers. Cara started to lay out her stuff next to Jesse when Kye put her towel down between them. She took off her black biker shorts and black tank top.

"Great suit!" Cara complimented Kye's neon orange bikini. Jesse thought she was going to be sick. Cara rarely complimented anybody, and here she was falling all over

Kye. Jesse knew it was going to be a long afternoon. The three girls lay down and put on suntan lotion.

"So, Cara," Kye began, and then with a look at Jesse, leaned over closer to Cara and whispered the rest of her sentence.

Jesse flipped over onto her stomach so she wouldn't have to appear as if she were listening. As if she cared what they were saying anyway.

Kye laughed loudly at whatever Cara whispered back, and turned over quickly, showering Jesse with a spray of sand.

Jesse sat up quickly. "Hey!" she yelled. "You got sand all over me!" She started brushing her legs off.

"Sorry," Kye said flippantly. "It was, like, an accident." She turned back towards Cara.

"Anyway, Cara," Kye continued, "when you come visit me in New York we'll have to go to all the cool stores down in the Village. There's this place called the Antique Boutique where you can get the best secondhand clothes—"

Jesse tried to tune them out while she picked the sand grains out of her lotion.

"It's totally cool . . ." Kye went on and on. "And there are amazing jewelry stands on the streets where they have really cheap silver earrings. You'll *love* them! I got these for five bucks," she said, pointing to the silver daggers hanging from her ears.

"I don't have pierced ears," Cara said, wondering why Kye hadn't noticed earlier.

"Are you *kidding*?" exclaimed Kye. "Why not? Aren't you allowed?"

"Of course I am," Cara lied. "I just never really wanted holes in my ears. What's wrong with that?"

"Sure," mumbled Jesse. "She's been begging her parents for years."

"What?" Kye said, turning to Jesse.

"Oh, nothing," Jesse retorted, getting up and heading for the water. She was going to have to go in the water to get the sand out of her sticky lotion. Cara and Kye didn't seem to miss her though. They were deep in conversation when she got back, so Jesse just pulled out a magazine and started reading.

"You want me to go get some sodas?" Cara asked, getting up.

"Sure," Kye said. "I'll come with you."

"Do you want something, Jess?" Cara asked, making it clear that Jesse wasn't invited to come along.

"I'll take a Coke," Jesse said, as she watched the two girls walk towards the food stand. Jesse could not understand what it was about Kye that made Cara act this way. Meanwhile, Kye was totally obnoxious as far as Jesse could see.

Kye and Cara returned about twenty minutes later, without a soda for Jesse.

"We lost it," Kye said, nudging Cara. Cara started to giggle.

"I forgot," Cara admitted, trying to stop laughing. "I'm sorry, Jess."

"No problem," Jesse answered curtly. "I'm not thirsty

anyway.'' Kye began talking about New York again, and Cara listened raptly. Jesse didn't know how much more she could take. Then, two guys who looked about twelve or thirteen years old walked in front of the girls. Their eyes lingered on Kye for a moment.

"Hey, dork-faces!" Kye yelled after them. "What do you think you're looking at?'' Cara started laughing as if it were the funniest thing she had ever heard. Jesse wished the sand would open up and swallow her—towel and all. At the very least, Jesse wished she could move her blanket away from them. That was so rude of Kye. Whatever possessed her to say that, Jesse wondered.

"This is really boring,'' Kye proclaimed a little while later. Jesse was totally relieved. The afternoon had been stretching endlessly before her.

"Well, let's go to Scoops,'' Cara suggested.

Kye agreed, and they all packed up their stuff. Jesse hadn't been asked if she wanted to go, but she didn't care. She just wanted to go home.

"I have to get home,'' Jesse said quickly as they walked back to their bikes.

"Why, Jess?'' Cara asked. "Come on. It'll be fun.''

"Right,'' Jesse muttered. "I've got to get home,'' she repeated, with no other explanation. Cara usually had to know every last detail about everyone else's life, but this time she didn't even ask why Jesse was in such a rush.

"That's too bad,'' Kye said, a smirk on her face.

"Yeah, well, see you guys,'' Jesse said, as she jumped on her bike and pedalled furiously away from the beach.

Later, after scooping up the last bit of ice cream in

their Scoops Saturday Special, Kye suggested going to the mall.

"Sure," Cara agreed. "That sounds like fun. I haven't been to Unique yet."

"And you could get your ears pierced," Kye suggested, although it came out sounding more like a command.

"Maybe," Cara said, stalling. She wondered how she'd get out of it. Luckily, Kye didn't bring it up again on the way to the mall. And she seemed to have forgotten all about it when they got inside.

"Let's go to every store," Kye suggested.

"Sounds good to me," Cara agreed, even though she thought it was the most ridiculous idea she'd ever heard. Besides, it would take hours.

The girls took the escalator up to the third level. They turned right and stood in front of a hair salon.

"Pretend you want to make an appointment to dye your hair black," Kye whispered to Cara as they walked in the door.

"No way," Cara hissed, but as soon as the lady asked if she could help them, Kye pushed Cara forward.

"Uh . . . I . . . um . . . would like to dye my hair," Cara stuttered, as Kye walked over to a table covered with barrettes, combs, ribbons, and all sorts of hair accessories.

"What color, dear?" the hairdresser asked, looking up at Cara. "But you have such beautiful hair. Why in the world would you want to change it?"

"Uh, I don't know. My friend told me it would look nice black," she said.

"Black?" the woman exclaimed. "You should definitely think that over. I don't think black would suit you. But if you decide that's what you really want, then come back."

"Okay," Cara said politely, as she turned around and grabbed Kye. She pulled Kye out of the store. As soon as they got outside, they burst out laughing. The next store was a lingerie shop. Cara was embarrassed just to be in there. She hoped no one she knew could see her. Kye picked up a red lace camisole and brought it over to the register.

"Do you have this in green?" Kye asked, looking totally serious.

"Uh, I don't think so," the sales clerk replied.

"Are you kidding?" Kye said, raising her voice. "What is it with stores in Florida? In New York, these come in green, orange, magenta, any color you want. Let's go," she declared, turning to Cara. Cara could hardly control her laughter until they left the store.

"I can't believe you did that," she said, giggling.

"Hey," Kye interrupted, changing the subject. "There's the Unique Boutique. Let's go there next," she suggested.

"But we'll miss the next four stores," Cara said, confused. Kye was the one who had said they had to go to *every* store.

"Change in rules," Kye announced as she ran over to the store, with Cara trailing right behind her.

Kye started walking up and down the aisles in Unique, pulling clothes off the racks as she went. After Kye had gathered up an armful, she told Cara to wait and then headed off toward the dressing room. Cara wandered around. She had never seen such wild clothes—in such neon colors. Cara didn't think they were quite her style, though. Then again, maybe they were. She *was* changing her image, with Kye's help. She was no longer the goody-goody she had been before Kye came to Palm Beach. And Cara kind of liked that, especially since other people were beginning to notice.

"I didn't like anything," Kye suddenly said, startling Cara. "Let's get out of here."

"You tried on *all* those things and didn't like any of them?" Cara asked in surprise.

"Right," Kye replied shortly. "Come on, let's go."

"Sure," Cara quickly agreed, but Kye had already started walking out.

"Let's go down a level," Kye commanded, walking over toward the escalator. "I have something I want to show you."

"What?" Cara wanted to know.

"Wait until we get downstairs," Kye hissed. Cara fell silent as the escalator carried them down.

"Come look," Kye said when they found an empty bench. She opened her bag and pulled out a black and white barrette, a big comb, and a black T-shirt with UNIQUE emblazoned across the front in neon green letters.

Cara was stunned. She hadn't seen Kye *buy* anything. "Where'd you get all that?" she asked.

"Where do you think?" Kye asked.

"You stole it?" Cara almost whispered. "I never even noticed."

"Of course not. That's the point," Kye said slowly, as though she were speaking to a five-year-old. "Otherwise you get caught. Haven't you ever shoplifted before?"

"No," Cara mumbled, wondering why she felt stupid for not having stolen anything before.

"Well, it's time to try," Kye declared in such a way that Cara knew she was helpless to say no.

"Why?" Cara asked, protesting weakly. She really didn't want to shoplift. What if she got caught? She was already grounded.

"It's a challenge," Kye replied. "Come on, it'll be fun."

"I don't know," Cara said, trying to stall one last time.

"Come on, Cara. Don't be such a baby," Kye complained. "I thought you were cool."

"I am," Cara replied, wondering just how cool she was. "All right," she finally agreed. "Where?"

Kye pointed to a large pharmacy across from where they were sitting.

"I'll wait here," Kye said. "Otherwise, they might get suspicious."

Cara walked slowly toward the pharmacy. Her palms were sweating and her stomach felt like it was full of

Mexican jumping beans. What was she doing? She also wondered why Kye wouldn't go in the store with her. It might have helped to have some support. She didn't really want to do this, but she didn't want Kye to think she was too chicken to try. Cara walked slowly up and down the aisles of the pharmacy, wondering what to take. At the far end, in the last aisle, was a large counter of nail polishes. Cara picked up a couple of bottles and pretended to read the labels. She looked around nervously, her hands shaking so much she was afraid she'd drop one. Then, when she was satisfied that no one was looking, she quickly slipped one into her shorts' pocket. Then she put the others down, walked over to the magazine section and picked up the latest *Sassy* magazine. She flipped through it so she'd just look like she was browsing. Then she put the magazine down, and walked quickly out of the store. She did it! Cara couldn't believe that she had actually gotten away with it. She was still expecting someone to come up behind her and ask her to empty her pockets.

"What'd you get?" Kye asked, when she got back to the bench. "Did you get anything?"

"Shhh!" Cara hissed, as she led Kye over to the stairs that led out of the mall. She wouldn't say anything else until they got outside.

"Okay, you're safe," Kye said sarcastically. "They're not about to follow you outside. Now, what'd you get?"

Cara held out the nail polish. It was black. She hadn't even looked at it before she put it into her pocket. It could have been any color.

"Nice color," Kye commented. "Not bad. Next time you'll have to get something bigger."

"I better get going," Cara said, hoping there wouldn't be a next time where shoplifting was concerned. That was all she needed, to get caught stealing. She was grounded already, and if Dora found out that she'd been gone all day, she'd be in a lot of trouble. Luckily Dora had the day off, but Cara didn't want to take any more chances. And if Dora found out about the black nail polish, she would raise the roof. "I'll see you at the car wash tomorrow, right?" Cara asked, as she hopped on her bike.

"Yeah, if I decide to show," Kye said casually. "By the way, you don't want that nail polish, do you?"

"You can have it," Cara replied, glad to be getting rid of the evidence. She would never use it anyway. Cara stared after Kye as she rode away. She had never had a Saturday quite like this one before. Kye was so different from her other friends. She took so many chances. Cara thought it would be really cool to visit her in New York over the summer, and finally see the Village. Cara couldn't get over how exciting it was to hang out with Kye. Definitely a thrill a minute. Yet, at the same time, something didn't seem quite right.

CHAPTER
11

"Hey, Quinn," Alicia called out. "We didn't think you were going to show up. We were getting worried." The parking lot at PBP was packed with sixth and seventh graders from PBP and G. Adams. They were all getting ready for the S.A.M.S. car wash.

"I know," Quinn replied, pulling her red hair back into a ponytail. "Neither did I. I forgot I was supposed to watch Patrick today. My parents went to some great aunt's funeral and didn't want to bring Pat with them. I couldn't bring him here. I'd never get anything done. Luckily, Sean said he'd watch him. Now, though, I owe him one."

"Oh, no," Esme said dramatically, giggling. "Last time you owed him one, you had to let him get that girl he liked to baby-sit for you for an entire night. Just so Sean could casually walk in and ask her for a date."

"Yeah," Quinn agreed. "It was pretty embarrassing, having a baby-sitter at twelve."

"So, where's Kye?" Alicia asked, suddenly changing the subject. "Everyone else is here."

"I bet she doesn't even show up," Esme predicted.

"Really," Nicole agreed. "She doesn't seem to have much school spirit."

"You guys aren't going to believe this," Quinn said, pausing to find a sponge and rinse it out. "But when we studied together the other night, I caught her copying my homework."

"What?" Nicole exclaimed.

"Yup," Quinn said. "And then she tried to tell me it was no big deal. She also said that I was a goody-goody for caring that she copied. Then she ran out saying she was right about me all the time. Can you believe it?"

"What a jerk!" Alicia said, filling a bucket with soapy water.

"Yeah, a total loser," Esme added. She picked up an empty tool apron with large pockets in front. She tied it around her waist. Esme was taking the money for her group because she didn't want to get all wet. She was wearing a new outfit—white overall shorts with a pink T-shirt, pink sunglasses, and a pink and white striped painter's cap. Esme had an outfit for every occasion.

"You know what I heard?" Nicole asked, searching for a spare sponge.

"What?" Quinn asked. Nicole always heard everything. They called her the Source.

"Jesse went to the beach with Kye and Cara yesterday.

She said Kye was really obnoxious to her and Cara would barely talk to her at all," Nicole said.

"But I thought Cara was grounded," Alicia interrupted, uncoiling a hose. "How could she go to the beach?"

"I don't know," Nicole admitted. "Jesse said they were supposed to go to Scoops afterward, but she couldn't take it anymore. She just went home and let Kye and Cara go alone."

"Let's put these signs up," Quinn interrupted. "We don't have much time." She propped up the big sign that Esme had made. It had the Students Against Multiple Sclerosis symbol in big, bright letters, and underneath it listed the prices for the car wash.

Quinn heard a boy's voice yelling behind her. "Get moving, McNair, or you'll get soaked," he shouted. She turned to see Jonathan standing there pointing a hose right at her.

"You wouldn't," Quinn said, seriously.

"I most certainly would," Jonathan said, also keeping a straight face.

"Jonathan Stanton," one of the G. Adams teachers called from across the parking lot. "We need that hose over here immediately."

"Yes, sir," Jonathan called back. Then he turned to Quinn and said with a sly grin and a wink, "You better watch out later."

"You, too, Stanton," Quinn threatened, but she couldn't help laughing as he walked away.

Five minutes later, the first cars started to arrive. Everyone broke up into groups of six to work on each car. One person took the money, one hosed the car down, and four people soaped and sponged.

The third car to drive up was a royal blue 1967 Firebird convertible. The girls almost died when they saw who was in it. Mr. Holmes was sitting behind the wheel, wearing cut-off jeans and a red T-shirt.

"Wow, he looks really good!" Esme whispered to Alicia. He certainly looked different than he usually did in the jacket and tie he wore every day to school.

"Great car," Quinn complimented. "I hope you've asked all your friends to come."

"You bet," he replied. "And I hear almost all the faculty will be here—even Mrs. Hartman."

"Great," Quinn replied sarcastically. She couldn't wait to see her favorite headmistress.

After Mr. Holmes left, the girls worked steadily for a few hours. Quinn, Alicia, and Nicole were covered with soap and Quinn felt as if she'd taken a shower, she was so wet. Her sneakers squished at every step. Suddenly Quinn stiffened.

"Miss McNair," Mrs. Hartman barked, as she rolled down the window of her black Mercedes. "You girls are out of uniform on school property."

Quinn stood perfectly still, her mouth hanging open in surprise. She was just about to protest when she saw Heartburn smile.

"I think I'll let it pass this time, though," the headmistress added. "You are doing a great job." She paid

Esme and rolled up the window, pulling her car down to where a group of kids were waiting to wash it.

After that, they took a quick break for lunch, and the cars kept lining up. The afternoon flew by. Sean showed up in his old bomb, with Patrick in tow. He said he'd told all the guys in his band to come, too.

When the last car had been cleaned and dried, Esme ran to put up a huge "CLOSED" sign. Alicia and Peter collected all the money from the different group leaders and went to count it. Quinn started emptying the water buckets and gathering them together. Suddenly, she felt a soaking wet sponge hit her back. She whirled around quickly.

"Jonathan Stanton, I'm going to kill you!" she yelled when she saw him standing behind her, laughing hysterically.

"I dare you!" he said.

"You asked for it!" Quinn declared, walking closer. She lifted a bucket full of soapy water and threw it at Jonathan. But he was too quick and jumped out of the way. Cara was walking behind Jonathan at exactly that moment, though, and the soapy water hit her right in the face.

Quinn's mouth dropped open. She hadn't been aiming for Cara, but she couldn't have planned it any better if she had tried. Everyone started laughing. Cara looked furious.

"I'll get you for this, Quinn McNair," Cara yelled as she shook out her dripping hair. The day, so much fun for everyone else, had been total torture for Cara. A soaking was the last straw. First, Kye didn't even show up. Then Jesse, Stephanie, Patty, and the others were really cold to her. She couldn't understand why they were treating her like that. Now, she was sopping wet, and everyone was laughing at her.

"I didn't mean it," Quinn called after her, trying to stifle her laughter. "I swear . . . I didn't—" but Cara had gotten on her bike, and was almost out of sight. Quinn fell over in a fit of giggles.

"Sure you didn't mean it," Jonathan accused, grinning.

"I wish I had thought of it," Alicia cut in, laughing so hard that she had tears streaming down her face.

"Don't worry, Quinn, she deserved it," Stephanie yelled from behind the lemonade stand. For the first time that any of them could remember, Jesse didn't jump to Cara's rescue. Jesse had had about as much fun as Cara. They had sold a lot of lemonade, and there were a lot of guys there. But Jesse had had a hard time keeping a smile on her face. She hated not being on good terms with her best friend. Still, Cara more than deserved the silent treatment.

Finally, everyone was finished cleaning up, though no one seemed ready to leave. They were having too much fun.

"Hey," Alicia called to Esme, who was standing with some of the guys. "How about a Super Deluxe Pizza-rama Special?"

"I'll be there in a minute," Esme replied, turning back to Bobby.

99

"I think this is the first time I've seen Esme delay eating," Nicole exclaimed with a grin. "She never puts anything before food."

"Now, *someone's* more important than pizza," Quinn said, staring over at the group. She wondered where Jonathan was. She hadn't seen him since she had tried to dump water on him, but she had kind of hoped he'd stick around. No matter where she was working that day, she had been aware of where he was.

"Are you guys ready yet?" Esme asked as she ran over to join her friends. "I'm starved!"

"Hoover!" Quinn yelled, playfully punching her friend. "We've been waiting for you!" They got on their bikes and rode over to Pizzarama.

When they walked in, the place was packed. It seemed as if almost everyone who had worked on the S.A.M.S. car wash was there. They looked around for a seat, but every table was jammed full of kids.

"Hey, Nicole," Jonathan called to her from the back. "There's room here." He was sitting with Adrian, Virginia, Missy, Bobby, and some other kids.

Nicole looked at him in surprise. Why was Jonathan being so friendly? One minute he was calling her stupid, and the next he was being sweet to her. She just didn't understand him at all.

"You guys want to sit over there?" Nicole turned to ask her friends.

"What do you think?" Esme asked, giggling. "*Bobby's* there!"

Alicia nudged her as they went to join the others.

Quinn blushed a little as Jonathan moved over and made room for her to sit next to him. Quinn didn't know where to look. She felt herself getting warm all over when her leg brushed against Jonathan's by mistake.

"I can't believe Kye never showed up," Missy commented. "Everyone else was there."

"She didn't strike me as the type who would wash a car," Jonathan said, chomping on an ice cube. Quinn tried to hide her smile. She had been worried when Nicole had told her that Jonathan had spent a lot of time talking to Kye at Cara's party. It was obvious now, though, that he hadn't been too impressed with her.

"Cara looked kind of lost without Kye," Virginia added. "Jesse and those guys weren't very friendly to her."

"And then Quinn practically drowned her," Jonathan said, looking serious.

"Did you see the look on her face?" Alicia asked, as everyone at the table broke up laughing.

"I still can't believe Kye wouldn't even help for a few hours!" said Virginia, when everyone had stopped laughing.

"That girl is more trouble than she's worth," Missy mumbled, as the pizzas arrived.

"Finally," Esme exclaimed, flashing Bobby a perfect model smile and pulling a huge piece of pizza off the tray.

CHAPTER
12

"You missed the car wash yesterday," Cara said to Kye as the two girls walked into school the next morning.

"So?" Kye replied. "Why would I want to hang out at school on a Sunday?"

"All the G. Adams guys were there," Cara added, trying to make it sound as if she had had more fun than she did. She was feeling a bit hurt that Kye hadn't shown up, or even called to tell her that she wouldn't be there.

"They're so immature," Kye retorted. "I had better things to do."

Cara wondered what Kye had been doing all day, but she didn't want to ask. What else would Kye have to do? Cara thought she was Kye's friend. She knew Kye didn't have any other friends in Palm Beach.

After grabbing their books, they walked into their homeroom. They made a beeline for the back of the room to sit side by side in the corner.

"My aunt is freaking out about my grades," Kye confided. "She said that if I don't do well on tomorrow's math test, she'll have to discuss my grades with my father. She also said he'd probably want me grounded for the rest of the term. Right!" She snorted. "That'll be the day."

"I could help you study," suggested Cara, glad to be back in Kye's confidence. "I'm good at math."

"Thanks," Kye said. "But there's no way I could learn all that stuff by tomorrow. I need some sort of guarantee that I'll pass that stupid test."

"What do you mean?" Cara asked, looking confused. The bell rang just then, and homeroom began before Kye could answer the question. Cara was left wondering what she was up to this time.

During math class that afternoon, Kye whispered across the aisle, "Cara, let's go to Scoops after school."

"Okay," Cara agreed, nodding quickly. Ms. Bauer was reviewing for the test, and Cara was having a little trouble following one of the problems.

When the class ended, Ms. Bauer's desk was surrounded by students asking last-minute questions about the test. Kye grabbed Cara's arm and practically pulled her out the door.

"Let's go, I'm starved," Kye said, almost dragging Cara towards their lockers.

"Don't you want to study?" Cara said, questioningly.

"I do, I do," Kye said. "But food definitely comes first."

Cara hesitated. She really had to study for this test.

For some reason, though, she couldn't tell Kye no. "Okay," she agreed. "But only for a little while, and then I really need to study."

"Oh, I forgot," Kye said suddenly, stopping midstride. "I promised Ms. Bauer I'd drop off the rest of last week's homework in her office before the end of the day. Will you walk down there with me?"

"Sure," Cara said agreeably. The math office wasn't out of the way.

"I've never been in here before," Kye said as they walked into the office. "Is anyone around?"

"No, why?" Cara asked, glancing around. "That's Ms. Bauer's desk over there."

"Thanks," Kye said as she pulled out a blank sheet of notebook paper and left it on the teacher's desk. As Cara turned to leave the office, Kye picked up a copy of the test from the pile in Ms. Bauer's "in" box and shoved it in her bag.

"We're out of here," Kye said, hooking her arm through Cara's, and practically skipping down the hall. "You want to come to my house?" she asked.

"I thought we were going to get ice cream," Cara said in confusion. How could Kye have forgotten about that? She just asked her. "And then we were going to go study."

"I have all the help I need right here," Kye whispered, patting her bag as they walked out the front doors of the school into the late afternoon sun. "Ms. Bauer saw to that."

"What do you mean?" Cara asked, turning to look at

Kye. Now she was really confused. Kye hadn't asked Ms. Bauer *one* question during the whole review.

"I mean that she happened to leave about forty copies of the test in a pile on her desk, and *I* just happened to borrow one," Kye replied with a sly grin.

"You what?" Cara gasped. "You mean you *stole* the test."

"And you helped," Kye said, laughing. "I couldn't have done it without you."

Cara was speechless. She couldn't believe that Kye had actually stolen a copy of the test and *she* had helped her! This was serious. Cutting school was not even in the same league as stealing a test. Kye could get kicked out of school. And so could she, because she had helped. Cara didn't know what to say.

"It's not such a big deal, Car," Kye said, blowing it off. "Now are we going to get something to eat or what? I'm *starved!*"

"Sure," Cara answered distractedly. Kye chattered the entire way to Scoops, but for once Cara tuned her out. She still couldn't believe that Kye had stolen the test. Up until that moment, Cara had really believed that Kye had gotten kicked out of those New York prep schools because of their stupid rules. But now she wasn't so sure. Things were getting more and more out of Cara's league every day. And she didn't know what to do.

Cara remained silent even after they got to Scoops. Kye ordered a banana split for them to share. Kye didn't even notice that she was doing all the talking.

Cara finally came to a decision just as Kye finished up the last of their ice cream. Kye would have to return the test. That was all there was to it. Kye could study with her all night if she had to, and pass the test tomorrow. She didn't need to cheat. Now all Cara had to do was persuade Kye to take the test back.

"Um, Kye?" Cara began.

"Yeah," Kye said, looking around Scoops. "Oh, no! Look who's here!"

Cara followed her gaze and saw Quinn and Sean walk in. Great, she thought. That was all she needed. Quinn *and* Sean.

Cara turned her attention back to Kye. "Kye," Cara began, "I really think you should return the test."

"What? Are you crazy?" Kye exclaimed.

"I can help you study," Cara pleaded. "You can pass. You don't need that test."

Kye snorted. "Cara," she began, speaking very slowly. "Why would I do any work if I didn't have to?"

Cara suddenly felt herself getting angry at Kye. What could she say that would make Kye return the test? "What if I tell?" she asked.

"You can't," Kye retorted, angrily. "If you do, you'll be in just as much trouble as I will be. What's with you, Cara? I thought you were cool."

"I can't believe you," Cara practically screamed. "Don't you realize how serious stealing a test is? This has nothing to do with being cool!"

"Hey, you've got to look out for yourself," Kye replied loudly. "Because no one else will. And if you were smart, you'd look at the test, too. Anybody could use an easy A."

"I can get an A anyway," Cara yelled, losing all control. "Cheat if you want, but I don't want anything to do with it—or with you!" Cara jumped up from the table and ran out of Scoops, her eyes filled with tears. Kye calmly licked the last of the ice cream off her spoon, paid the check, and walked out of the restaurant.

Neither Cara nor Kye had noticed that Quinn and Sean had sat at the booth right behind them and had overheard their entire fight.

"Did you hear that?" Quinn exclaimed, looking over at Sean as Kye walked out.

"How could I miss it?" Sean asked in surprise.

"I can't believe Kye stole the math test," Quinn said. "I mean, I know I caught her copying my homework and all, but this is totally different."

"It's pretty serious," Sean admitted.

"I wonder how Cara knows about it," Quinn mused. "I don't think she could have had anything to do with it."

Sean started telling Quinn about some seniors at his school who had stolen a final once, and the whole class had seen it. Everyone had to take the class over that summer.

"Sean, what should I do?" Quinn interrupted him. She couldn't just let this go. It was completely dishonest.

"I don't know, Quinnster. This one you're going to

have to work out for yourself,'' was all the advice he would give.

Quinn sat there quietly. She didn't want to tell Ms. Bauer or Mrs. Hartman about it. Whatever Kye might think she was, she definitely wasn't a tattletale. She would have to figure out something. The problem was that she really had no clue as to what to do.

CHAPTER
13

"Good thing we're seeing a movie in class today," Esme said with a yawn. She, Nicole, Alicia, and Quinn were walking to their first period class.

"You'll probably sleep through the whole thing," Alicia said, and groaned. "You sleep more than anybody I've ever met, and you're always tired in the morning."

"Can I help it if I need lots of sleep?" Esme defended herself.

"Lish, you know these models need scads of beauty sleep," Nicole teased.

Nicole and Alicia giggled. Esme pretended to pout. Quinn didn't seem to be paying attention at all. She looked as if she were moving on automatic pilot or something. She was having a difficult time keeping her mind on what her friends were saying. All she could think about was the stolen test. What was she going to do about it? The test was today—she didn't have much time to decide.

"What's up, Q?" Alicia asked, noticing Quinn's unusual silence. They had just slid into their seats in history class, and Ms. Gordon was setting up the movie projector, so everybody was still talking.

Quinn looked up, startled. "Uh, nothing," she said quickly. Sean was right—this was something she had to figure out by herself. Quinn couldn't involve her friends in this. It was *her* problem.

"Come on, Quinn," Alicia persuaded, not giving up. "I know you better than that. What's bothering you?"

Quinn was rescued by Ms. Gordon turning off the lights and starting the movie. Quinn didn't mean to hurt her friends, but she really had to figure this out herself.

The day passed much too quickly. Quinn spent lunch hour in the library studying for the test so she didn't have to avoid her friends' questions. But she still hadn't figured out what to do. She had to think of something so she wouldn't have to tell Ms. Bauer.

Sitting in math class last period, Quinn still racked her brain. She knew that she had to concentrate on math now and worry about the stolen test later, but she couldn't stop wondering what to do.

Quinn wasn't really surprised to see Cara walk in and sit down in a seat as far away from Kye as possible. Cara was in the front row, and Kye was behind Quinn in the last row. Then Cara got up to talk to Patty, who was sitting a few aisles away. Kye walked up to the front of the room to sharpen her pencils. Quinn watched as Kye slipped a folded piece of paper into Cara's notebook on her way to the sharpener. Kye must be feeling badly about their fight, Quinn thought. She probably wrote a note trying to make up or something. If Kye lost Cara as a friend, she wouldn't have too many left—if any.

Ms. Bauer walked in with a stack of tests.

"Good afternoon, class," she greeted them cheerfully. Quinn wondered why teachers had to be so cheerful on test days. Maybe they were happy that they didn't have to teach that day or something. But Quinn felt she could really do without all the jolliness. "Open your notebooks and take out some work paper. You're going to need it."

Very encouraging, thought Quinn. As she opened her looseleaf binder to get more paper, she saw Ms. Bauer bend down to pick up the folded piece of paper which had fallen out of Cara's notebook. Ms. Bauer started to hand it back to Cara, but froze mid-motion. She slowly unfolded the paper.

"How did you get a copy of this?" Ms. Bauer asked Cara. Quinn didn't think she had ever heard her sound quite so angry.

"A copy of what?" Cara asked blankly. She stared down at the paper in Ms. Bauer's hand. Cara knew right away that it was the stolen math test! How did it get in *her* notebook? Kye must have done it. Cara felt her palms beginning to sweat. She had no idea how she was going to get out of this one. "I—I—don't know," she stuttered.

"You *don't know* how a copy of the test ended up in

your possession, Cara," Ms. Bauer said sarcastically. "I find that very difficult to believe."

"But, I didn't take it!" Cara protested. She couldn't very well tell Ms. Bauer that Kye had taken it, since she had been there. And then Ms. Bauer would just want to know why she hadn't told anybody sooner. What was she going to do?

Ms. Bauer looked sternly at Cara. "The evidence seems to indicate otherwise, Cara," she said. "I think we had better go to see Mrs. Hartman." She turned to the shocked class, and said, "I'll send someone in to proctor the class. Good luck on your test, girls."

The class sat in stunned silence after Ms. Bauer and Cara had left the room. Quinn turned around to see how Kye was taking all this. She was picking her nails, with a satisfied smirk on her face. Quinn couldn't believe it. The nerve of that girl. Quinn was going to make sure that she faced the music for this one.

She didn't have a chance to think about it further, though, as Mr. Holmes walked in and passed out the test. Quinn took a few deep breaths and stared at the paper in front of her. She had to concentrate on math now and worry about this other stuff later.

The test wasn't too bad after all. Quinn handed her paper in, and resisted the idea of talking to Mr. Holmes about the stolen test. She couldn't just pass the problem on to him. She walked slowly to Mrs. Hartman's office. She would have to let Heartburn know that it wasn't Cara who had stolen the test. But how could she do that without telling her that Kye was the real culprit?

The headmistress's door was closed when Quinn arrived. She sat down on a bench to wait. Soon the door opened and Cara ran out, crying. She didn't even glance at Quinn. Quinn stood up and walked over to the door. Ms. Bauer was still standing there, talking to Mrs. Hartman. Taking a deep breath, Quinn knocked. The headmistress looked up, startled.

"Miss McNair," she said in surprise. "What can I do for you?"

Ms. Bauer got up to leave. "I'll talk to you about this later," she said.

Quinn stopped her. "Please stay, Ms. Bauer. I need to talk to you, too."

Ms. Bauer looked at her curiously. Mrs. Hartman raised her eyebrows in surprise and sat down.

Quinn took a deep breath and exhaled slowly. Here goes nothing, she thought. "Cara didn't steal the test!" she blurted out quickly.

"How do you know that?" Heartburn asked, her eyes narrowing.

"What do you mean?" Ms. Bauer asked, shutting the door. Quinn felt like she was about to be interrogated. Next they'd sit her in a chair, turn on some bright lights to make her sweat, and hit her over the head with question after question. Maybe this hadn't been such a hot idea after all.

"Sit down, Miss McNair," Mrs. Hartman ordered. Quinn's palms felt sticky. The lights were next. "Now, tell me what you're talking about."

"I know that Cara didn't steal the test," she said again.

"Well, then who did?" Ms. Bauer asked. "And how did a copy of it wind up in her notebook?"

"Well," Quinn began and then stopped. This was going to be complicated, she thought. "I saw someone put something in Cara's notebook before you came in, Ms. Bauer. And I know this person is the one who took the test. I heard her say so."

"And who might that be?" Mrs. Hartman asked, leaning forward across her desk.

"I really can't tell you," Quinn confessed. Heartburn looked ready to kill.

"What do you mean, you can't tell me?" she asked, frowning.

Quinn swallowed, and repeated to herself that she was doing the right thing. She wasn't doing this for Cara. She certainly would never thank Quinn for it. But Kye had gone too far this time. "Well, she didn't exactly tell me that she stole the test," Quinn admitted. "I overheard . . . this person . . . uh . . . talking . . . talking about having it yesterday."

Mrs. Hartman's eyes narrowed. Ms. Bauer came to Quinn's rescue. "I have an idea how we can find out who took the test without forcing Quinn to point the finger," Ms. Bauer said, smiling at Quinn. "I didn't really think Cara was capable of stealing a test. I mean, she's a good math student, and she doesn't need to cheat."

"Okay, Ms. Bauer," Mrs. Hartman agreed. "It's your class; I'll leave it up to your judgment." She turned to

Quinn. "Thank you for coming forward, Quinn. You may go."

Quinn turned to leave. "Thank you, too, Quinn," Ms. Bauer said. "Please don't tell anyone that you've been here. I want to catch this culprit unawares."

Quinn nodded her agreement, and walked out of the office. She felt as if a great weight had been lifted off her shoulders. But she still couldn't tell her friends about the whole mess. She knew she should wait until everything had been cleared up. Quinn hated keeping secrets from her best friends.

"I can't believe Cara *stole* a test!" Patty exclaimed.

"There's no way she could have," Jesse defended.

Jesse, Patty, Mimi, and Stephanie were waiting for their pie at Pizzarama after school that afternoon. They were discussing the afternoon's events.

"There's no way she would do anything like that," Jesse continued. Jesse had no clue why she was defending Cara. Cara had totally ignored her for the past two weeks, and even been kind of nasty. But Jesse felt that it wasn't all Cara's fault, somehow. Kye had very definitely influenced her. In fact, Jesse wouldn't be at all surprised if she found out that Kye was behind this whole test thing.

"Well," Stephanie began as their pizza was put down in front of them. She paused to grab a slice and take a bite out of it. "Ms. Bauer found the test on the floor next to her desk, Jess," she said, reaching across Mimi to grab a handful of napkins.

115

"I was there," Patty said. "It definitely fell out of Cara's notebook. Why would Cara have a copy of the test if she didn't take it?"

"I don't know," Jesse admitted. "But I bet Kye had something to do with it." She barely noticed when Patty put a slice on the plate in front of her.

"Are you sure you're not just saying that because Kye is Cara's best friend now?" Stephanie asked reasonably. "I mean, I definitely don't like Baldwin, but before we start blaming her, we should know the facts."

Jesse didn't need to know the facts to know that Cara couldn't have had anything to do with it—no matter how she had been acting the past few weeks. She just would not steal a test, no matter what anyone said, or what Ms. Bauer found.

"Aren't you going to have any pizza?" Mimi asked Jesse, looking down at the untouched slice in front of her.

Jesse glanced down blankly. She really wasn't hungry. She decided to go home and wait for Cara's call. Somehow, Jesse knew that Cara would call—and that she would need her to be there. After all, she was her real best friend, Kye or no Kye.

"Good afternoon," Ms. Bauer greeted her class cheerfully the next day.

Quinn sat up straight in her seat. She pulled some blank paper out of her looseleaf binder.

"Please clear your desks, class," the math teacher instructed. "And take out some work paper."

"What?" the girls exclaimed all at once.

"We had the test yesterday!" Virginia said. "Why are we having it again today?"

Ms. Bauer smiled. "There was a bit of a problem yesterday, so to clear it all up, and to be fair, we're taking a new test today."

"It's not *fair*!" Kye exclaimed from the back of the room. "You didn't warn us about another test. You can't do this!"

"Of course I can," Ms. Bauer replied. "You don't have any problem with this, do you Kye? It's on the same exact material. If you did well on yesterday's test, then you'll do just as well today. It's nothing to worry about."

Kye muttered something about hating the stupid school, and then she shut up. Quinn smiled to herself. She thought the whole thing was totally rad—to use one of Esme's surfing expressions.

Meanwhile, Cara was in shock. Did this mean that they had believed her when she said that she didn't steal the test? Mrs. Hartman had mentioned suspension yesterday, but then nobody had contacted her parents about it. Something must have happened after she left the office the day before. She felt better than she had for a while. And last night Jesse had said that things would get better. Cara hadn't believed her then, but, well, maybe she was right.

The next morning Quinn was late for homeroom. Her bike had gotten a flat tire, and she'd had to go back and

117

get Sean's. Of course, the seat was up too high, and she couldn't get it to budge. She tried to ride it the way it was, but her legs wouldn't reach the pedals. Finally the seat moved down, but when Quinn jumped on, one of the tires was flat. Then she'd had to wheel it to the gas station around the corner to fill the tire with air. When she finally made it to homeroom, she was surprised to see everybody still running around.

"You're not going to believe this," Alicia whispered excitedly to Quinn as soon as she walked in the door. "Kye is leaving PBP."

Quinn could believe it, but she wasn't about to let on. "What? Why?" she asked innocently.

"Well, Patty heard that it really was Kye who stole the test, and Cara had nothing to do with it. Heartburn decided that Kye was definitely more trouble than she was worth, and expelled her from school. I think she went back to New York, or something."

Kye was the subject of conversation all day. She had been kicked out of PBP and had gone back to New York to live with her father.

Cara was relieved that Kye had gone. Sitting in her room after school that day, she realized just how much she'd been in over her head. Kye had totally overwhelmed her. Cara had never really known anyone like her before, and for a while it had been really exciting to hang out with her. Cara was ashamed that she hadn't stopped when things started getting out of hand. Cutting school, shoplifting, cheating—none of it was that cool.

She couldn't imagine why Kye was the way she was. Why did she have to do all those stupid things? Obviously, friends didn't mean much to her, after the way she had framed Cara. That was really low. Cara still couldn't believe that she had done that.

Well, if nothing else, Cara thought, she had learned something from this. She was never going to let someone else control her like that. And she would be very careful about choosing new friends in the future. The only thing she regretted was that she had never gotten to see the Village, or find out what it really was.

The doorbell rang, interrupting Cara's thoughts. She heard Dora answer it and greet Jesse, Stephanie, Mimi, and Patty. Cara was more than happy to have her old friends back. She didn't know what Jesse had said to them, but she was glad that they'd come over. She jumped up, and ran downstairs to meet them.

The next morning, Cara was her old self again.

"Nice socks, Quinn-o," Cara said sarcastically. "You must hit all the garage sales or something."

Quinn looked down at her gold glitter socks. She had to admit that they were much flashier than her usual, and she would never tell Cara, but she had gotten them at the Salvation Army. Quinn thought they were kind of cool—really mod, very Seventies. But who was Cara to make fun of her socks?

"They are just so tacky," Cara couldn't resist adding. She put her nose in the air and walked away, leaving Quinn with her mouth open, standing by her locker.

Kye had barely been gone a day, and already Cara was

acting the way she always used to. In a way, Quinn thought, it was kind of nice to have the old Cara back. At least she was predictable. Quinn grabbed the rest of her books from her locker and shut the door. She walked down the hall towards her first period class, smiling broadly.

Watch for UPSTAGED
next in the Palm Beach Prep series

"Y ou guys," Alicia said, slowing down until she was barely moving. "We're almost there. I'm not ready."

"Come on, Lish," Quinn encouraged, giving her a friendly push. "You're as ready as you'll ever be. So Trey is actually going to submit his music video to the video contest on MTV?" she asked, brushing a stray strand of red hair out of her eyes.

"All I know is that last night when I was listening to WKLX, Spike—that DJ Esme has a crush on—said that Trey London would be at Scoops on Saturday at noon to sign up girls for the basement video he's producing," Alicia explained, and then stopped dead in her tracks. "What if I wrote down the wrong day, or what if it was earlier and I missed it!" she cried, her black eyes dark with worry.

Quinn went ahead and peeked around the corner. "I don't think you have the wrong day," she commented, walking back to where Alicia, Esme and Nicole were standing.

The girls kept walking. "You definitely have the right

day," Nicole said, and pointed toward Scoops. There were girls hanging all over the place.

"Caramba!" Alicia exclaimed.

After they had sat down at a booth at Scoops, a tall skinny guy with blond hair and green eyes, who was fighting his way through the door, started talking above the noise of the crowd. "Okay, girls," he drawled, "I know you all want to be first, but just get on line and we'll take you all one by one." He was wearing a white T-shirt, black jeans, and a black blazer. His blond wavy hair hung down past his shoulders and he had a diamond stud earring in one ear. It was pretty obvious from the way he was moving that he thought he was pretty hot.

"That's him!" Alicia whispered excitedly. She straightened her miniskirt and sat up straighter.

"What an attitude!" Quinn exclaimed.

"He dresses pretty cool, though," Esme put in. "Black is very L.A., you know."

Alicia ran her fingers nervously through her black curls. "I guess I'll go and get on line to sign the list," she said.

"Go for it, Lish!" Quinn said.

"Really," Esme and Nicole said in unison.

Alicia smiled at her friends and then started to walk toward the long line of girls. She moved slowly up the line until there was just one girl ahead of her. She snuck a peek at Trey. She had to admit that, attitude or not, he was really cute. And after all, he must be really talented since he was the son of Rain London, the famous guitarist.

Finally, it was her turn. Alicia pulled the sign-up paper toward her across the counter, and her heart skipped a beat. It was already full on both sides. This didn't mean it was too late, did it?

"Excuse me, Mr. London," Alicia said, looking over at Trey.

"Hey, babe, you can call me Trey," he said, his green eyes boring into hers. Alicia suddenly had the urge to pull her miniskirt down so that it went somewhere below her knees.

"There's no more room on this paper," she continued, trying to sound as if trying out for a music video were something she did every day.

"Well, why don't you come over here and get another piece of paper," Trey suggested with a small smile.

Alicia's heart jumped into her throat. Trey looked totally gorgeous when he smiled.

"You a singer?" Trey continued, moving closer to Alicia.

"Yes," Alicia answered as calmly as she could.

"Play anything?" Trey went on, his eyes still fastened on Alicia.

"A little piano," Alicia answered, glad that her mother had forced her to take those piano lessons.

All of a sudden, a loud and sickeningly sweet voice started calling, "Treeeyyy!!!!"

Alicia didn't even have to turn around to find out who it was. She knew that voice only too well. Before she could even finish filling out her name, Cara had sauntered over to Trey and started flipping her blond hair all over the place. Alicia glared at Cara. She should have figured Knowles-it-All would want the part, too. The weird thing was, though, that Alicia and everyone else at PBP knew that Cara couldn't sing to save her life. But she sure looked serious about getting into the video. Alicia would just have to knock all their socks off by singing as she had never sung before . . .